SUGAR CREEK GANG

THE TREE HOUSE MYSTERY

SUGAR CREEK GANG

THE TREE HOUSE MYSTERY

Paul Hutchens

MOODY PRESS • CHICAGO

ISBN: 0-8024-4835-6

Printed in the United States of America

1

IT WAS ONE of the rainiest days I ever saw.

If it *hadn't* been a rainy day, I might not have been browsing around in our big *New Merriam-Webster International Dictionary*, which we keep upstairs in the alcove of our south bedroom.

If I *hadn't* been browsing around in the dictionary just to give my mind something to do—and also to keep from losing it—I wouldn't have stumbled onto the very exciting idea that was to give the gang a flying start into one of the strangest experiences we'd ever had.

Without that exciting idea, we wouldn't have built the new tree house I'm going to tell you about right now, and also about the mysterious stranger who moved into it one night without our permission, and landed us into the middle of one of the saddest stories there ever was, part of which actually happened to us but most of it to the old stranger himself.

Before there was any sadness, though, there was a lot of gladness, and the six members of the Sugar Creek Gang were right in the middle of everything—all the mystery and hot-tempered action, the disappointments and the brand-new kind of danger, the kind of danger that makes a boy feel fine to be in the middle of—like a boy feels fine to be racing along in the center of a whirlwind, dodging this way and that, running in a zigzagging fashion out across the pasture, not knowing where he is going nor when he will stop.

Actually, it took two ideas to get things *really* started. The first one came flying into my mind from page 2,386 in the dictionary, and the other came in through my left ear, when I answered the telephone about seven minutes later.

Browsing around in the dictionary is one of the most interesting things I ever do around our house on a rainy day—especially when Dad is away from home. When *he* is there, *he* gets to the dictionary first—and there isn't room enough for two people in front of a dictionary at the same time—or as Dad says to me sometimes, "Move over, son; your small mind is crowding me," trying to be funny and not being very.

It had been thundering a lot and lightning all kinds of the prettiest lightning you ever saw, some of it being what Dad calls just plain "sheet" lightning, and some of it "chain" or "forked" lightning, tearing like mad across the Sugar Creek sky.

About fifteen minutes after the thundery part of the storm was over, the rain settled down into a lazy drizzle that anybody who knows his rain knows is the kind that sometimes lasts all day, and it's hard to keep from feeling grouchy in that kind of weather.

Well, as our family does with nearly everything around our place, we had given our dictionary a name, calling it "Aunt Miriam"—its actual full name, as you know if you have one like it, being *The Merriam-Webster New International Dictionary, Second Edition.*

Many times when Mom is wondering where Dad is and can't find him anywhere else, she makes a beeline for our upstairs south bedroom and finds him in the alcove with "Miriam," working a crossword puzzle or just moseying from page to page, picking up new things to think about. "My mind gets awful hungry," Dad often says jokingly to Mom, and then adds, "and my wife is a bum cook!"

Mom herself spends quite a lot of time with "Aunt Miriam" every week, when she is studying her Sunday school lesson—being a teacher of the Gleaner's Class. Maybe a thousand times I've heard Mom say, " 'Miriam' has the most interesting ideas to make the lesson come to life."

I guess I was feeling especially grumpy that rainy afternoon, not being able to go outdoors or be with any of the gang like I wanted to. Mom was sitting sewing near the east window in our living room, getting as much light as she could from the murky sky. Charlotte Ann, my sometimes-cute baby sister, was pestering me to give her another piggyback ride, and I didn't want to do it. I'd already walked and run and crawled all over the whole downstairs with her on my back—and also on my shoulders—maybe a half dozen times that afternoon. Now I wanted a little peace and quiet for my mind, which was very hungry and trying to get something to "eat" out of a new book my parents had bought me for my birthday.

So when Charlotte Ann kept on fussing and tugging at me, I yelled at her, “Scat, will you! Leave me alone!” I swung around in my chair, turning my back on her, and started to let my mind sink down into one of the most interesting books I had ever owned. It had in it over a hundred colored pictures of American birds with interesting facts about the bird families they belonged to. A lot of the birds were the kind that lived and moved and made their nests around Sugar Creek.

There were quite a few long words in the book, and it was fun to learn the meaning of them. Two of the words were especially important to anybody who wants to learn about birds. One of the words is *altricial* and the other *precocial*—but “Aunt Miriam” knows exactly what they mean.

The *precocial* bird babies, such as ducklings or chickens or grouse or shore birds, are born with down or fuzz on them, and are able to run around to find their own food soon after hatching.

But most baby birds are those called *altricial* and are hatched completely naked, and all their food has to be carried to them, they are so helpless.

I was thinking as I sat, straining my eyes in the dark room, that Charlotte Ann was like an *altricial* baby bird. She’d had to be waited on hand and foot ever since she was born, and still had to be almost two-thirds of the time, or she wasn’t happy. She just couldn’t be baby-sat with but had to have something doing every second, and *I* had to do it.

If what I did seemed funny to her or made her happy, I had to keep on doing it, over and over and over again.

If only she would quit pestering me, I could do a little thinking, I thought. That's when I whirled around in my chair, and that's when I had to stop reading. As I whirled, my left foot struck against her chubby little legs, bowled her over and sent her sprawling onto the floor, where she let out a shriek and started to cry, her voice sounding like a loon choking on a half-swallowed fish. It only sounded a little bit like a human baby crying.

The unearthly cry coming from Charlotte Ann shattered Mom's peace and quiet and brought her voice to excited life. "Bill Collins! What on earth is the matter with you today! You certainly don't act very *sociable*!" she exclaimed, probably meaning she thought I ought to stop reading my interesting book about American birds and become a baby-sister-sitter by giving Charlotte Ann another piggy-back ride around the house.

The word *sociable* was a new word to me, coming from Mom like that, so I decided that as soon as the chance came, I'd go upstairs to the alcove to see what "Miriam" had to say about it—to see what kind of boy I *wasn't*, and Mom wished I was.

Well, after I had baby-sister-sat for about another half hour, and Charlotte Ann still wasn't satisfied but got fussier and fussier, I, being on my hands and knees at the time, tumbled her off my shoulders onto the floor—sort of accidentally, maybe—and exclaimed to her, "You are the most altricial bird

I ever saw. What on earth's the matter with you, anyway! Why don't you grow up!"

But of course a baby only two years old couldn't get any older all of a sudden. Mom decided she was "fussy-sleepy" and needed her nap, so we put her into her pink Scottie-dog bed in the downstairs bedroom and shut the door—and I was free to do what I wanted to for a while.

"Where you going?" Mom asked when I started toward the kitchen to go through it to the stairway.

"Up to see 'Aunt Miriam,'" I answered, which is the same thing Dad always says when he is going up to look up something. "My mind is half starved and my mother is a bum cook."

"Can't you stay down here to keep me company?" Mom asked with an accusation in her voice. "It's a very gloomy day."

"I'm sorry," I said back to Mom by the window, "but I don't feel very *sociable* this afternoon," thinking maybe I already knew what the word meant. I kept on going toward the stairs, expecting any second Mom's voice would lasso me and make me come back to mother-sit a while, but when I climbed all the way up to "Aunt Miriam's" alcove without being stopped, I decided Mom wasn't going to be a helpless mother that had to have attention on a rainy day.

I stood looking down at "Miriam" on her little roll-away table and thought how nice it was that she was always ready to let a boy know almost anything he wanted to know. She was always open, even when nobody was using her, on account of that was part of the instructions that had come with her when Dad bought her: we were always to leave her open with about the same number of pages on either side; it was better for such a large book to be kept like that.

First I lifted the purple scarf Mom had made for her, so her staying open like that wouldn't make her a dust-catcher, because dust is not good for an open book.

In a jiffy now, I would know what kind of boy I was supposed to be, and wasn't. I'd find out what Mom had meant when she said, "You certainly don't act very *sociable.*"

Before looking up the word, I rolled "Miriam's" table over to the rain-spattered south window where there was more light, and stood for a long minute looking down and out through the curtain of falling rain at the puddles in the barnyard and up at the excited clouds still scudding across the sky like they were disgusted with life and didn't care who knew it, like they would rather be sailing around high and dry, far up in a beautiful sunshiny blue sky. Even the clouds looked grumpy and felt so bad they were crying about it, I thought.

Grumpy clouds, a grumpy boy with grumpy memories! That was the way I felt that very minute. Through the window that was catching all the rain's tears it could and draining them off onto the ivy leaves below, I noticed the pignut trees up at the end of the garden, tossing around with the half mad wind, and remembered something every exciting that had happened in the clover field up there.

That topsy-turvy experience had been caused by a new boy who had moved into our neighborhood, a boy named Shorty Long whose blue cow had upset the calm of the whole territory. I had fought several times with Shorty, and in at least one of the battles in which he had bashed my nose, I had given him a licking. I had also been licked myself at the end of that same fight.

"Ho hum," I sighed through the window at the rain. "At least I won't have to worry about the short, fat Long boy this summer!" The family had moved away; Shorty's blue cow, Babe, was also gone, and as far as we knew there wasn't a single boy enemy left to cause us any trouble.

But, I thought right that second, *what boy wants that? What he really wants is to be in the middle of some kind of excitement.*

Still not ready to look up the word I had come to look up, I lazied to the unpainted, cedar, attic door and opened it just to listen to the rain on the shingled roof. That was one of my favorite sounds—rain on our attic roof, or on our barn roof when I'm up in the haymow. Rain on a shingled roof makes a boy feel sad and glad and lonesome all at the same time, like seeing and feeling a baby rabbit trembling in the palm of his hand.

Pretty soon I was back in front of "Miriam," turning her big rectangular pages to the word *sociable*.

"So *that's* what I'm not," I said aloud when I saw what Miriam said Mom had said I wasn't very. "I'm not very 'friendly,' I am not 'inclined to seek or enjoy companionship with others of the same species.' "

"Mom is wrong," I said to me. "I'm one of the most sociable persons in the world—when I'm with the gang."

My mind reached out its arms and gave a great big sociable hug to every other member: Big Jim with his almost-mustache and powerful biceps; Little Jim, the littlest member; Dragonfly, the spindle-legged member, who is allergic to ragweed in hay-fever season and sneezes at almost every strange smell; Poetry, the barrel-shaped member and my almost-best friend, who likes poetry almost better than most boys like blackberry pie; Circus, who has a beautiful singing voice, and when he grins, looks more like a monkey than any of the rest of us.

Right then my eyes stumbled onto something especially interesting. It was a picture of a bird perched on a branch of what looked like a large toadstool—only it wasn't a toadstool. It was, "Miriam" explained, a huge bird's nest. The bird was what is called an African sociable weaverbird "which breeds in colonies, nesting in one great umbrella-shaped structure of grass placed in a tree."

I looked in Dad's encyclopedia and learned that sometimes as many as a hundred or even two hundred pairs of sociable weaverbird parents work together to build a giant-sized grass house with hundreds of small nests in it, and the birds all live together without fighting.

For some reason, right that second, it seemed I ought to be willing to give my own sister a few extra piggyback rides without complaining. Maybe I could even help the whole Collins family build a more friendly home.

Just as I was wheeling "Miriam" back to her place in the alcove, I heard the phone downstairs ring, and my mind leaped into hope that whoever was calling would be one of the gang, one of my very own "species."

I hadn't any sooner reached the end of the banister at the head of the stairs, getting ready to plunge down, than Mom's cheerful voice came singing up to me, "Bill! Telephone!"

I was out of breath when I reached the phone, after a stormy dash down the stairs, through the kitchen, and into the living room and across its many-colored rag rug to the east window, where the phone was fastened to the wall.

"Who *is* it?" I whispered to Mom, and she whispered back with her hand over the phone's mouthpiece, "He sounded very businesslike." Her eyes had a twinkle in them that said the person on the other end of the line was one of the gang. Mom liked all the members almost as well as I did.

I used a very businesslike tone of voice myself as I spoke. "The Theodore Collins residence, William Jasper Collins speaking."

A second later I knew who had called me—and it was good old squawky-voiced, mischief-minded Poetry himself, my almost-best friend. He was in a cheerful mood. "Is this the Sugar Creek Tent and Awning Company?" he asked.

"It's the Sugar Creek *Everything* Company," I

answered, using an even more dignified voice than he had, and feeling proud of myself for thinking what I thought was a bright remark.

"This is Leslie Thompson's father's boy. I'm speaking for his son. Do you repair old lawn umbrellas? The storm has ripped ours to shreds and we have only the metal ribs left."

And *that* is when the *second* idea hit me—the one that was to get this story really started. With my mind's eyes I saw the whole thing—the Thompson's large lawn umbrella converted into the roof of a grass tree house for the gang to meet in. We would cut the top out of a young sapling down along the creek or the bayou, lash the umbrella's center pole to its trunk, then interweave blue grass and timothy and some of the tall sedge of the marsh near the swamp, tying everything together with binder twine, maybe covering the metal ribs of the umbrella with chicken yard wire first. When we were finished, the roof of our house would look like an African sociable weaverbird's monstrous nest.

To keep out the rain and wind, we'd have to have sidewalls which we could make out of pieces of old canvas from some of our dads' harvesters.

"We certainly *do* repair old lawn umbrellas!" I almost screamed into the phone. "We certainly do. Bring it right over as quick as you can!"

And that was *that*—the beginning of the gang's new grass-roofed hideout, which we actually built, using the skeleton of Poetry's folks' old lawn umbrella for the framework of the roof. When we finished it, it didn't look any more like an African sociable weaverbird's hundred-family tree house than the man in the moon looks like a man. It was a pretty nice house, though, and was a good hideout for us to hide *in* from our imaginary enemies. Its roof was actually rainproof and whenever there was a rain coming up and we knew it, we would run helter-skelter for its shelter and stay as dry as a feather in the sunshine. We even outfitted it with some old furniture.

We used our tree house for our headquarters for all kinds of explorations into what we pretended was wild Indian country; also we actually acted out the Robinson Crusoe story we all knew so well.

But it was only make-believe, and a boy can't be satisfied all the time with a lot of let's-pretend stuff. Once in a while something has to come to some kind of life, which nothing did except that a lot of birds—some *altricial*, and some *precocial*—thought our nest was full of wonderful material for making their own smaller nests, so they kept stealing the straw and sedge and stuff, which we had to replace or our roof would leak.

But still nothing happened, day after day after day. Nothing *real* until—

I say nothing happened *until*—By "until," I mean *not* until the day we found the mysterious old stranger living in our house. If we had known who he was and what kind of adventure he was going to lead us into, we probably wouldn't have decided to let him keep on living there. We might have been scared to.

2

WE HAD BUILT our tree house on a knoll between the bayou and the slope leading down to the creek where there was a good place to fish. We'd had a hard time deciding just where, at first, because Old Man Paddler, who owns the woods and most of the territory around our playground, was away on a trip to California to see his nephew, and we kind of hated to cut the top out of a sapling on his property without his permission, even though we were pretty sure he'd let us.

So, when we found the very strong, just-the-right-sized young tree on the grassy knoll, which was on Dragonfly's folks' bottom land, we built it there.

The house wasn't much to look at after the walls and the roof turned brown. When Mom herself saw it, which she did one day when she was down along the creek with her camera, she said, "It looks like an old brown setting hen on a nest," and she snapped a picture of it.

The first we knew anybody had moved into it, was one very hot afternoon while Old Man Paddler was still on his vacation in California, and we were sort of lonesome for him—his own cabin up in the hills looking sad and lonely, too.

"Let's go take a look at our old setting hen to see if she has any chickens under her," Little Jim said, with his cute mouse-like voice. And away we all went, from the spring where we were at the time, zip-zip-zip through the giant ragweeds in the path toward the swimming hole, which led past our tree house.

All of a sudden, Dragonfly, who was ahead of the rest of us at the time, called, "Hey, you guys, somebody's had a fire here."

The big surprise came a few fast jiffies later, when Dragonfly yelled to us from inside our thatch-roofed house, "Hey! You birds come here! Somebody has moved into our house and is living here!"

In a fleeting few seconds there was a scramble of flying bare feet carrying the rest of us to where Dragonfly was, where we quickly funneled our way inside, looking around to see what Dragonfly had seen, which wasn't much, only an old brown suitcase, and a few cans of different kinds of food on our little folding table which we had put there to eat on, and the camp cot on the far side.

Then Dragonfly's crooked nose sniffed suspiciously, and he exclaimed, "I smell turpentine," and sneezed to prove he had.

I'd been smelling it myself, although I thought it was paint of some kind. The odor was hardly strong enough for anybody except Dragonfly to notice it, not any more than you could smell if you walked up to the trunk of the big ponderosa pine that grows beside the path on the way to the sycamore tree, and smelled the yellowish, sticky fluid that oozes from it.

Dragonfly sneezed again and squeezed his way past me to the exit, sneezing twice before he could get outside into the fresh, pure air. But he hadn't been outside longer than it would take him to sneeze twice more, when he hollered again, this time, saying "Hey, Gang! Somebody's coming!"

Then I heard it myself. Somebody or something *was* coming.

Would we be caught snooping around, looking over somebody's private property? It seemed we ought not to be there, even if it was our very own tree house somebody had moved into.

"I'm getting out of here!" Circus exclaimed, and was the first to duck out, with the rest of us following like bumblebees storming out of their nest after a boy has poked a stick into it.

We fanned out in six different directions, but mostly in the direction of the spring which was the very opposite from the direction of the sounds. As soon as I felt we were out of sight, I stopped and listened.

At first there was only the sound of the worried water in the Sugar Creek riffle, and a half dozen robins scolding in the trees overhead and all around, accusing us of trespassing on robin property, saying "Quick! Quick! Get out of here, Quick!"

I was used to hearing Robin Redbreast and his family scolding like that, on account of nearly every summer for years a pair of them had built their nest in a crotch in the upper branches of the plum tree in our yard.

Even though birds didn't belong to our species,

still we ought to love them and not destroy their nests. It seemed, though, that if we sort of accidentally trespassed on what they thought was their own property, they ought to be a little more sociable about it.

How we had all gotten together so soon after our helter-skelter scramble from our birdhouse, I don't know, but there we all were, crouching in the grass of another small knoll behind the shrubbery, panting and serious-faced and excited and wondering what on earth, and who.

Just then Dragonfly, who was crouching beside Little Jim and peeking through the foliage of a sweetbrier bush, sneezed, maybe on account of the extra sweet smell of its leaves and flowers, and whispered, "Look! I see him! He's a—he's a Negro!"

I was so surprised at Dragonfly's tone of voice, that I looked at his face, and it seemed he actually looked insulted, as if a black person wasn't as much a human being as he, Dragonfly, was.

My parents had taught me that people of other races were as good as white people, the same as robins were as good as meadowlarks, which happen to be of a different color. The One who had made the robins and all other birds, had also made the different-colored human beings. The color of a person's skin wasn't important—it was the kind of heart a person had that counted, Mom had said many a time.

So when Dragonfly said what he had just said in the tone of voice he had used, I felt my temper getting ready to catch fire.

Maybe I ought to explain that there were very few black families in Sugar Creek territory. The one we knew best was named Ballard; the father's name was Samson, and everybody called him Sam. He was one of the kindest men anybody ever saw; and he was a hard worker, with muscles as strong as the village blacksmith's in a poem we studied in school; and he made a good living for his family.

My eyes galloped after Dragonfly's, and I saw what he saw, and sure enough the person was black. He was walking with a limp, using a cane, and heading straight for our tree house door, coming from the direction of the spring.

"Look!" Dragonfly whispered again. "He's got a bottle of something!"

I was seeing the same thing. Dragonfly was right. The man did have a bottle.

I saw something else too. I saw the old man raise his hand to his head like he wasn't feeling well, sway a little, and sort of sink down on the grass. Then he fumbled in a shirt pocket for something, took it out, poured something into his hand, and put it into his mouth. Then he lifted the bottle—shaped like a whiskey flask—to his lips and took a drink. I knew it was an actual whiskey flask, because I'd seen quite a few lying along the roadside, and sometimes even down at the spring on Monday morning when there had been Sunday picnickers in the woods. Whiskey bottles make good targets for a boy's slingshot, if you set them up on a fence post.

"He's trespassing on our territory," Dragonfly said. "Let's go order him off."

We'd seen enough when we'd been inside our house a little while before, to know that the man had actually moved in. How long he had been there, we didn't know, but he'd stayed at least one night.

We couldn't keep on crouching there in the grass, doing nothing, so, pretty soon, Little Jim who was next to me, suggested, "Why don't we all start whistling and talking and moseying along toward where he is, and see *who* he is and if we can help him some way."

A jiffy after Little Jim suggested that, Big Jim made it an order, and a few seconds later, with all my nerves tingling and my heart pounding for wondering what on earth, I was following along with the rest of the gang, all of us trying to act like ordinary boys doing ordinary things, just rambling along the creek with nothing on our minds except being happy on a sunshiny afternoon.

That is, we started to start, but Dragonfly stopped us with a bossy "Wait! You guys stand back of me! I'm going to order him off our property!"

"Why?" Big Jim wanted to know. "What's he doing wrong?"

"Trespassing," Dragonfly answered with a set face, then added with a loud whisper, "He's a Negro!" And when he said the word, there was what looked like a sneer on his face.

I just couldn't believe it! A member of the Sugar Creek Gang feeling like Dragonfly's tone of voice said he felt right that minute!

My thoughts were interrupted right then, because

something started to happen beside and behind me. It was Circus and Dragonfly having a scuffle, with Circus shaking Dragonfly by his shoulders and saying, "That old man is *not* trespassing. Nobody is trespassing on anybody else's property unless there's a sign that says No Trespassing, and besides, he's a human being, the same as you are—only maybe more so!"

Big Jim stopped the scuffle with his voice and his powerful muscles, pulling the boys apart and saying, "There's doesn't actually *have* to be a No Trespassing sign. But if we all say he's *not* trespassing, then he isn't."

I was glad there wasn't going to be any rough-and-tumble battle between two members of our gang, though I knew their thoughts were still fighting, even if their muscles weren't. I was also proud of Circus for feeling the way he did. He was one of the best thinkers in the whole gang, and always made good grades in school; he was especially good in arithmetic which I sometimes wasn't, and he had one of the best boy-soprano singing voices in the whole territory, sometimes singing solos in church.

A boy as fine as Circus couldn't help it that he had six sisters and hardly ever got a chance to help his mother with the dishes, like a certain other boy I know gets to do.

But this wasn't any time to let myself feel sorry for myself for being the maybe best boy dish-washer in the territory. *What*, I asked myself, as the robins, which had been scolding that we were trespassing on *their territory*, calmed down a little—*what* would happen during the next few minutes?

3

WHILE WE WERE topsy-turvying along toward the very bald, very black old man, who just that minute took another drink out of his flask, a lot of things were tumbling about in my mind. In my imagination I was sitting in our one-room, red-brick schoolhouse, during what is called Opening Exercises, which we have every morning.

Sometimes for Opening Exercises we listen to our teacher, Miss Trillium, read from a fiction story, sometimes we listen to a recording of music by some famous musician—things that are supposed to be good for boys and girls to know about.

But the morning I was remembering right that minute, Miss Trillium had written the words of a gospel song on the blackboard and was teaching it to us, letting us learn it by singing it ourselves. First she sang it with her own contralto voice, then she asked us to sing with her, which we did, singing or squawking or growling or whining along. The other members of the gang were in their different seats beside, behind, and in front of me; only Poetry, home with a cold, was missing. Scattered in other seats were nine girls who also came to our school.

Girls also belong to the human race and sometimes are smarter than boys, but they can't help it.

In a little while I had the words and the tune of the song in my mind, and was making a vocal noise with the rest of the school on it:

> Jesus loves the little children,
> All the children of the world;
> Red and yellow, black and white,
> They are precious in His sight,
> Jesus loves the little children of the world.

When we finished singing the chorus for the last time, Miss Trillium said something I would never forget as long as I lived, and it seemed the most important thing a boy could ever know. I can't remember exactly what she said, but it was something like this: "Let us always remember that all human beings are the handwriting of God, and The Creator writes with different colored inks—sometimes red, sometimes brown, sometimes black, or yellow, or white. All human beings are His creation, and all are souls for whom Christ died."

Miss Trillium finished her quiet talk by adding, "Let us learn to see God's handwriting in all people. He knows that a man's worth is not determined by the color of his eyes or hair or skin. He looks upon the *soul* of a man—not just his outward appearance, and since He loves us all, should we not also love one another?"

All those thoughts went scurrying through my mind as fast as a chipmunk scooting across the open space between the Black Widow stump and the leaning linden tree.

Poetry, beside we whispered, “Red and yellow, black and white—”

Big Jim took over for us then, calling out politely, “Good afternoon, sir! Is there anything we can do for you?”

The old man reached for his cane, holding onto it tightly, like if he had to, he could use it to protect himself.

I got a surprise then, in fact a shock, when all of a saucy-voiced sudden, Dragonfly called out from about ten feet behind us:

“Do you know you’re trespassing on private property? My father owns the land that house is built on, and the whole house belongs to the Sugar Creek Gang!”

The old man winced as if someone had struck him in the face—only I knew instead, Dragonfly had stabbed him in the heart with harsh words. He looked about at his belongings: his cane, his small brown suitcase, then into the house at the few things he had there.

My own eyes took in the pint flask out of which he had been drinking, and which he was holding in the palm of his right hand.

Another thing I noticed was that in his other hand he had a tiny bottle with some very small pills in it. Whatever was in the flask was so transparent it could easily have been water.

Little Jim must have been thinking what I was, because right then he whispered in my ear, “It’s a medicine bottle. I'll bet he's got heart trouble, or something."

For a second after Dragonfly's insulting remark, not a one of us said a word. It was like there'd been a big explosion of some kind, and we couldn't talk; everything was so quiet, except for what Little Jim had whispered to me.

The old man must have been really shocked, because he looked very sad for a minute. Then he raised his right hand and waved it in the air like a boy in school does when the teacher has asked a question and the boy wants to answer. This is what his trembling voice said in answer to Dragonfly's insult: "I'm sorry if I trespassed on your property, boys. But it was chilly and rainy last night, and I—well, I did sort of move in. I'll be glad to pay. How much for one night?" He fumbled in his left hip pocket, and drew out a billfold. When he opened it, I saw bills and bills and *bills!*

"You don't owe us anything," Big Jim answered for all of us. "Not a single red cent." When he had said it, I noticed a frown on Dragonfly's forehead. He was looking and *looking* at the bulging billfold.

"But I'd really like to pay. Here. Take this. It would have cost me much more if I'd stayed in a hotel or motel." He counted out five one-dollar bills and pushed them toward us.

Again Big Jim answered without bothering to look at any of the rest of us, "If you want to stay another night, that'll be all right, too, but we'd rather not charge anything."

A very grateful expression came into the old

man's brown eyes. He looked us all over from head to foot, then grinned a friendly, toothless grin. "I think I'd rather pay rent. As I said, I'd have had to pay at a hotel or motel. I tried to get a room at the Green Corn up the road a piece, but they were filled up. Maybe they'll have a vacancy later in the week, but I *would* like to stay a few nights. It's closer to what I want to do." Again, his hands were busy with his billfold, and again he offered us money; and again Big Jim refused it, saying, "Not for last night, Mr.—Mr.—"

"Robinson," the trembling voice said, "Benjamin Robinson."

"Mr. Robinson, we'll talk it over to see if we want to accept anything, if you decide to stay longer. But—" and then Big Jim added something I'd never thought of, which was, "we don't have a license to run a motel, and we might get into trouble actually charging for our house."

Benjamin Robinson gave Big Jim a friendly look, and with a twinkle in his eye, maybe at the idea of our sociable weaverbird tree house being a motel unit, said, "Thank you, thank you very much." All of a sudden he began to open and close his lips very fast and to act like he was chewing something; then he said, looking around, "I've been talking all this time without my teeth. I'm sorry."

He drew from his jacket pocket a napkin, unwrapped a set of false teeth, and fitted them into his mouth.

Well, I'll speed up this part of the story for you so I can get started on what followed. We left the old man and went up to the cemetery for a very special meeting to decide whether to charge him rent.

We held our meeting like we do quite often in the grassy place not far from the tombstone at Sarah Paddler's grave, the one that has on it the chiseled hand with a forefinger pointing toward the sky and the words, "There is rest in heaven."

Dragonfly sat a little outside our circle with a pout on his lips, like he knew what we were going to decide and he was against it. He spoke first and said, "Did you see all that money in his billfold? I'll bet he had a hundred dollars! I'm going to charge him for every night he stays!"

"You *what!*" Big Jim almost thundered at him. "*You* are going to charge him! What d'you mean?"

Dragonfly's face got a mussed-up expression; he looked toward the sun to make it easier for him to finish the sneeze he felt coming, then sneezed twice and answered, "That house is on my father's bottom land!"

We had some hot words back and forth for a while, and finally, with his eyes blazing, Big Jim brought it to a vote. "All in favor of letting Mr. Robinson stay a week in our house free, raise your right hand."

All our kind-of-dirty right hands went up, except Dragonfly's. That stubborn-minded little guy spoke up saucily, saying, "We don't want any black people living in a white man's house!"

I'd hardly ever seen Little Jim fire up, but when Dragonfly said that, that quiet-faced little guy answered in a way to make me really proud of him. His short, sharp words came out like a lot of blazing arrows: “You can’t judge a book by its cover.”

Dragonfly’s eyebrows dropped, his forehead wrinkled into a frown, and I knew it was Little Jim’s words that had shut him up.

The vote being five to one in favor of letting the old man stay in our house, it meant he was going to stay.

Before our meeting broke up, though, we voted on one other thing, and it was that *if* the old man *wouldn’t* stay without paying us *something*, we’d take whatever he gave us and use it to buy books for our Sunday school library. That vote was five to one, also—Dragonfly wanting to divide the money between us, and wanting the old man to pay him one extra dollar a night, because the house was on his father’s land.

It was an interesting experience, having our house rented—for that’s what was finally decided. The old man was so sure we should accept something, so we finally agreed on ten dollars for the week he was going to stay.

That meant he’d have to have what is called “service,” so all of us—except Dragonfly—got busy, carrying firewood for a little outdoor fireplace which we built for him not far from the house, carrying spring water in a pail Poetry brought from his house, getting him a can opener for the canned food he had, and making the place as nice for him as we would have for any paying guest.

Late that afternoon, when I was in our haynow

throwing down hay for the stock, I climbed away up over the hay to my secret place near the crack in the log, knelt down for a while, and talked to the heavenly Father about what we had done. While I was on my knees in the sweet-smelling alfalfa, I began to feel wonderful inside, like God was talking to me, telling me we were right. I didn't actually hear any words, but a very cheerful thought was in my mind, *"I'm proud of you boys. I haven't anyone to represent Me on earth except people who love Me, and who do what is right."*

I went to bed that night thinking about something Dad had said to Mom at the supper table. I began to worry about it while I was lying there with the moon streaming in on my pillow, and it was hard to get to sleep. Over and over and over again the words went tumbling through my mind.

"The Gilberts have leased the Green Corn Motel up at Pike's Corners. They want to try the motel business to see how they like it. They had all the units taken last night except two."

The Green Corn Motel. The Green Corn Motel! Dragonfly's folks had leased the Green Corn Motel at Pike's Corners! The old man had tried to get a room there last night and there hadn't been any vacancies. Mr. Robinson would have had to sleep out in the open if he hadn't stumbled onto our empty sociable weaverbird tree house and had crept in there out of the rainy weather and the cold night air and gone to sleep.

There had been *two* vacant units at the Green Corn. *Two!* But the old man couldn't rent even *one*. Could it be because he was black? And Dragonfly's folks had told him they were filled up, when they weren't?

I lay there between Mom's nice clean sheets, listening to the different night sounds, such as the cheeping of the crickets outside, the whirring of the katydids saying over and over "Katy did; Katy, she did; Katy did; Katy, she did"; hearing the five-leafed ivy's hundreds of leaves whispering in the breeze at the window.

I tried to count sheep like they say you *should* do when you are having trouble falling asleep, imagining I was seeing a lot of snowy-white lambs in single file, leaping over the rail fence just across the road from "Theodore Collins" on our mailbox, and gamboling in a long line down the path toward the spring.

But always the lambs made a beeline for our tree house, and then I'd be more wide-awake than ever, hearing with my mind's ears Dad's words at the supper table.

Before I knew what I was going to do, I was sitting up in bed in the moonlight, with my fists doubled up. I must have said something out loud, on account of Dad called up the stairs saying, "Having trouble up there? Any reason why you can't keep quiet so your mother can go to sleep?"

Hearing that, I felt sad for a minute on account of Mom had been having such a hard time getting enough sleep the past few weeks. I certainly didn't want to keep her awake.

I sighed and lay down again. But the Green Corn

Motel's vacant units kept flying around in the sky of my mind. All the units were *black* with *white* windows, and they had false teeth.

And then, all of a sudden, it was morning, clear and cool and cheerful. As I looked at "Aunt Miriam's" innocent, open face across from me, and then out the window at the pasture and saw the dew drops glistening on the clover, I began to feel fine inside again.

But when I looked back at "Miriam," her pages still open to the picture of the sociable weaverbird nest, I didn't feel so happy. With our one homemade, one-room unit, we had gone into the motel business, and we had ten dollars in advance, which Big Jim was taking care of for us. Our unit had been built on Dragonfly's parents' property, and for some reason they didn't seem to like black people either.

Just then Mom called up the stairs in her usual before-breakfast voice, which is nearly always a singing voice, saying, "Breakfast's ready!"

At the table, Mom said to Dad, "Remember our rule about anything we don't like. We try to sing our complaints until after we've had coffee." Of course, Charlotte Ann and I didn't drink coffee, but milk or juice of some kind.

Dad had been frowning at the five shriveled pieces of bacon on his plate beside the two poached eggs. "I didn't say a word," he answered Mom.

"But your forehead was growling," Mom answered.

Dad began to sing then to the tune of the "Doxology" in our church hymnal, "Sing gaily while the bacon burns, Sing gaily while—"

Mom interrupted his song with words that didn't have any tune at all, "I'd like some roasting ears pulled for dinner, if one of you men would be interested."

The words "roasting ears" reminded me of "Green Corn," so I spoke up without any tune in my voice: "You say Dragonfly's folks have leased the Green Corn Motel at Pike's Corners?"

"Yes, they have," Mom answered, "and I'm afraid it's a mistake. The last couple who leased it lost hundreds of dollars."

Dad's answer was, "That's because they leased it in the fall *after* the tourist season was over, or nearly so. They couldn't make the rent. The Gilberts are good managers, and they'll probably make a go of it."

"I still don't think it was wise," Mom answered, and there was a scolding tone in her voice.

"What happened to the music?" Dad asked, and Mom quick answered, "I guess I'm a little low today. Don't pay any attention to how I say things. I'm sorry."

I was proud of the way Dad answered Mom, "That's all right, Mother. I don't feel so cheerful myself." He finished just as Charlotte Ann in the bedroom decided it was time for her to start *her* day without singing—and the morning was off to a kind of nervous start, with Mom trying hard all morning to be cheerful and not being, and a lot of things going wrong around the house, such as Charlotte

Ann deciding it was the right day for her to be cross and had to be baby-sat with almost half the morning.

Dad, however, was as chipper as anything, singing and whistling around the farm and barn. Every now and then when he came to the house for some reason, he'd go upstairs to see "Aunt Miriam." He was studying something special about animal husbandry. There were so many new words in the book he was reading and carrying around in his hip pocket, snatching thoughts out of it every now and then, that he had to have "Miriam's" help to understand it.

I guess I haven't told you yet that Dad was a little like Poetry; he was always memorizing what he called a "quotable quote." One he had quoted to us quite a few times that summer was, "He who never made a failure probably never made a discovery."

He and I were standing by the pitcher pump at the end of the boardwalk about fifteen feet from the kitchen door, when he quoted it to me that very morning. It seemed from the tone of his voice that he was going to mention some failure of *mine*, something I had done that day and shouldn't have, or *should* have done, and *hadn't*.

To change the subject, I asked, "You suppose Dragonfly's folks *will* make a failure?"

"I'm not as pessimistic about it as your mother," Dad said, then lowered his voice, put his arm across my shoulder, and added, "Mother's not feeling well, today, Bill. Let's be especially thoughtful, helping her all we can, and not paying any attention if she says anything sharp or cross. We know what a wonderful person she is, don't we?"

I certainly did know. I told him so, and he explained, "She didn't sleep well last night; and when a person gets only a few hours' rest, it's hard to be sweet the next day."

"I didn't sleep well last night, myself," I answered Dad, "so if I'm not a good boy today I hope you won't think anything of it."

I could feel Dad grinning behind my back, before he answered, quoting another quote, "The rest of your days depends upon the rest of your nights."

I decided to tell Dad about renting our sociable weaverbird tree house to Ben Robinson and why, and that fired up his temper in a way that made me proud of him, when he said, "You mean he'd have had to stay out in the chilly weather all night because the Gilberts wouldn't rent him one of their vacant units?"

Dad's jaw was set, I noticed, when I looked up at him. I thought he was going to sing something in what is called a minor refrain. Instead, he answered, "But the Gilberts *do* have a problem. Unfortunately, there are still in America a few prejudiced tourists who'd rather not stay at a motel which is integrated, which the Green Corn is supposed to be. It's a social problem that can't be solved in a day."

"You want to hear one of the best quotable quotes there ever was?" I asked.

"Surely, let's have it," Dad said, and I gave him Little Jim's quote which was, "You can't tell a book by its cover."

Dad didn't say a word for a few seconds. He took a sip of water out of the tin cup we always had hanging there on a wire hook, tossed the last half of the water into the puddle on the other side of the iron kettle, around which a lot of sulphur and white butterflies were drinking, scattering them in about seventeen different directions.

Then Dad pumped a drink for me. While I was drinking, I looked over the top of my cup and noticed the butterflies settling down around the water puddle again, and it was a pretty sight, their yellow and white wings opening and closing, opening and closing while they drank.

"Those butterflies used to be caterpillars, son. It must feel fine to be able to fly, after having spent a whole winter in a cocoon," Dad said in a lazy voice, then added, "They shouldn't have any difficulty being cheerful after all that sleep."

Dad gave me a half hug then, and I was glad I had him for a dad. We kept on standing there till nearly all the butterflies came back and were making a yellow and white border around the rim of the puddle, like a big wheel without any spokes. He must have felt that I was worried about the old man, and especially about Dragonfly feeling the way he did, and acting like a black man wasn't any more than a caterpillar to be stepped on.

"I don't like Dragonfly's folks very well," I said, "and I'm still mad at Roy." Roy was Dragonfly's real name, and I only called him that when I didn't like him very well.

"Look, son," Dad said in the tone of voice he always uses when he is teaching me something. "We won't judge the Gilberts until we know what they are thinking. Besides, we don't actually *know* they turned the old man away. Also I'm not sure they *could* do it even if they wanted to. Motel managers don't have that choice in our country anymore, but let me ask you a question. What if by allowing a black person to stay at the Green Corn, they would offend some of the white tourists, and they would move out? The Gilberts might lose a lot of money which they need very much right now. They've been having a hard time financially, and they're getting ready to spend a lot of money on their son for special allergy treatments—money they don't have."

My jaw was tight. I did like Dragonfly in spite of *not* liking him. I knew how Mom would answer a question like that, so I looked Dad straight in the eye and answered, "I think maybe God would take care of their money problems some other way." All of a sudden there was a glad feeling in my heart, like there had been yesterday when I was up in the haymow; and it was, *I'm proud of you boys. I haven't anyone to represent Me on earth, except people who love Me and who do what is right.*

It seemed like maybe God and I had a secret, and that He and I were special friends.

I was interrupted in my thought right then by my father putting his hand on my shoulder and saying, "Thank you, son, thank you every much. You put the will of God first in your life, *all* your life, and He will never let you down."

My cheerful feeling exploded all to smithereens

right then, when Dad astonished me with, "There's a lot of agitation over in the next county against black folks. There was a cross-burning at Sam Ballard's last night."

"What's a cross-burning?" I asked. I'd never heard of one. I was tense in all my muscles and scared.

Dad's answer didn't help me feel any better when he explained, "Some rough, tough, heartless young fellows set up an oil soaked wooden cross in front of Sam's house and set fire to it. It was their way of saying, 'We don't like you!' "

4

ALL THE REST of the morning, I kept thinking about Sam Ballard waking up in the middle of the dark night and seeing a flaming cross just outside his front door, and how scared he and his wife and children must have been.

I imagined one of their little-girl twins running to her mother and crying and asking how come there was a fire. For a few minutes, while I hoed in our garden, I let my mind swing me back through history all the way to the time when Jesus was here on earth, and the people who hadn't liked Him had nailed Him to a cross, and I saw the blood coming out of His hands and feet and from around the crown of thorns on His head.

I didn't realize I was singing until I heard my voice on the words of the gospel chorus Miss Trillium had taught us, "Jesus Loves the Little Children of the World."

The sad feeling in my mind changed to a mad one when all of a sudden I thought again about the cross-burning at Sam Ballard's house. Spying a Canada thistle growing at the edge of the garden, and knowing that if it wasn't cut down or uprooted, it would grow into a savage-prickled, three-foot-tall, farmer's enemy, and if enough of them got really started, they could take over a whole field. I raced across the garden with my hoe, chopped the thistle down, and dug out its roots.

While I was slicing away at that Canada thistle, it seemed like I was trying to chop out what my parents called prejudice.

The rest of the morning finally passed, and it was time for dinner. We were all at the table, about to bow our heads for Dad to ask the blessing, when Charlotte Ann, still not feeling very happy, decided she wanted to stand up in her chair, and did. At almost the same time, her blue mug of milk upset; the milk spilled out, flowed across the corner of the table, and fell splashing onto the linoleum beneath her chair.

A whirring second later, Old Mixy, our black-and-white cat, who was in the kitchen at the time, made a dive for the milk on the floor and started lapping it up in a hurry to drink as much of it as she could before Mom could mop up the rest of it.

"Scat!" I yelled down at Mixy, just as Charlotte Ann let out a baby-style blood-curdling wail.

Mom came to some of the fastest life I had ever seen her come to in my life. For maybe six minutes there was the most nervous excitement in our kitchen you ever saw or heard or felt—especially *felt!*

"When *will* that child learn she can't do that!" Mom exclaimed. "When *will* she stop trying to do acrobatic stunts at the table! Honestly, Theodore!" She finished with her eyes fixed on Dad at the head of the table.

Right then Dad quoted again one of his newest quotes, saying in a strong, calm voice, "He who has never made a failure, has probably never made a discovery."

"That wasn't a *failure*," Mom said in her very worst voice, making me feel sad inside. "*That* was just plain disobedience. We've taught her *not* to do it, and she knows *better* than to stand up in her chair! I don't care if it does make her feel big, to get up so high! She *knows* better."

"She only half knew it up to now," Dad answered quietly. "She just this minute learned the other half. I was reading this morning in one of Byron's poems, one of the finest quotes a family could ever learn. He said, 'Sorrow is knowledge.' "

"Byron!" Mom's voice barked. "He was never married and wouldn't know how to discipline children! He probably never expected anybody to quote poetry in the middle of a family storm!"

That wasn't the first time Dad had used that quote, but I would never forget it now; in fact, I used it myself that same week.

In a little while, our upset family was right-side-up again and ready to eat, but I could tell by the way I still felt inside, that even though the worst part of the storm in Mom's mind was over, there was quite a little thunder and lightning left and that Dad was still feeling like a small tornado himself. It seemed like everybody was to blame for everything except maybe Charlotte Ann, who was now tied into her chair and couldn't have gotten out or up, no matter how hard she might wriggle.

"Sorrow has taught her to sit still," Dad remarked. "Sorrow is knowledge."

I joined in the conversation by quoting Dad's other quote, "She who never made a failure, has probably never made a discovery."

Mom didn't act like she even heard. Instead, she said, "All the excitement made us forget to ask the blessing." She looked at Dad, who was what is called the head of our family—and most of the time was—and the twinkle that had come into his eyes when I had quoted his quote, went out like a firefly's flash fades a second after it is turned on.

A jiffy later all our heads were bowed and all our eyes closed except Charlotte Ann's, which, I noticed, were wide open looking at the ceiling where three or four flies were buzzing about.

Part of Dad's prayer was about Charlotte Ann herself, and for a minute it seemed he was almost bragging to God about what a fine baby she was, when he said, "Bless our dear little girl, so lively, so filled with childish enthusiasm, and so normal. Help us to know how to train her. Give Mother and me a little education for ourselves while we are bringing her up and while we are making so many failures. Help us all to make some new and very important discoveries as we live along the rugged road of life. Give us a greater love for Your beloved Son, our Saviour, for each other, and for people of every race and color."

I couldn't understand why all of a sudden Dad's voice began to choke like it had tears in it. He finished his prayer right away. When I opened my eyes again, his and Mom's were already open. They were looking at each other, their eyes had tears in them. Also, Dad's calloused right hand was on the table, clasped around Mom's kind of small hand, and I knew the storm in our family was really over, that Mom and Dad were the best pair of parents in the whole world.

Finishing my piece of freshly baked apple pie, I asked to be excused. Getting the nod from Dad, who at the same time got a nod from Mom, I was out of my chair and across the room to pick up my straw hat from the floor where I wasn't supposed to have left it, and was outdoors in a flash, going as far as the iron pitcher pump before I heard the screen door slam too loud behind me, and as far as the grape arbor and was swinging by my legs upside down before Dad's voice crashed into my peace of mind, demanding, "Come back here, young man, and correct your mistake!"

It was a new way of saying, "Come back here and close that door like a gentleman!" which order I had heard that summer as many times as there were sulphur and white butterflies ringing the puddle by the iron kettle. Dad's words scattered my peaceful thoughts in all directions, sending them flying all over some place or other.

My folks must have thought that as soon as I had closed the door quietly, which I did kind of fast, I would dash on out across the barnyard or somewhere else quite a ways from the door, but I didn't. I stayed there for a jiffy, just thinking, and that's how come I happened to overhear Dad say to Mom,

"We may have to try a little sorrow on our son. I'm afraid he's a little slow learning that screen doors *are not* firecrackers and that every day, a hundred times a day, it is *not* the fourth of July."

I went on back to the grape arbor, tested my powerful biceps by chinning myself a few times on the crossbeam; then I lazied out across the yard, past the plum tree, in the top of which Robin Redbreast and his wife had their nest; went on to the walnut tree swing, where with a half-innocent feeling in my mind, I opened the front gate and went through, shut it like a gentleman so the noise of the latch wouldn't hurt Mom's nerves; then I stopped.

My still innocent mind was urging me to go on past "Theodore Collins" on our mailbox, slowly cross the graveled road, then make a flying leap over the rail fence and go racing like a cottontail down the path toward the spring, where I hoped some of the gang might be waiting for some of the rest of the gang to come and play with them.

I was thinking and wondering about the old stranger too, wondering how he slept last night. It would be a good idea to see if there was anything he needed, such as a pail of water from the spring, or anything else.

Of my own free will—I *think*— I went back to the house, stopping about seven feet from the side door near the ivy arbor that shades the porch there.

"I almost made a mistake," I said to Mom and Dad, with a joke in my voice.

"You are a very bright boy," Dad answered. "The

discovery you are about to make is hanging on the towel rack by the dish pan."

Just that second I heard a cardinal calling from somewhere. Its voice was so cheerful, like a cardinal's voice always is, that my heart became as light as a feather in a whirlwind. I looked toward the top of the walnut tree, and there on one of the highest branches was a splash of red as pretty as the red hair ribbon one of Circus' many sisters wears to school.

Mom was up and out of her chair in a hurry, and standing at the screen door looking up at the walnut tree. A second later she exclaimed under her breath, "Oh, *oh!* Isn't he magnificent!"

Before Dad could get out of his captain's chair and to the door, there was a flash of red streaking across the sky, over our house roof to the other side somewhere.

Without thinking, I swung into a fast run and was circling the house in a hurry to get another glimpse of Mom's favorite bird, the kind that always made her happy just to see or hear it.

I found out how much the cardinal actually cheered up Mom about three minutes later, when I was on the west side of the house, standing near the rain barrel at the southwest corner, straining my eyes out into the orchard to see if I could catch a glimpse of fiery red in the foliage of one of the trees. Right away, I saw him, in the very top of Old Jonathan, my favorite apple tree.

Any minute now, I'd stop looking out into the orchard and would look down into the rain barrel half filled with yellowish-brown water caught from the last rain, and would see my reflection in it; then I would yell down into it just to hear the big round hollow sound it always made, that being one of my favorite sounds around our place.

That is when I heard Mom's voice coming through the open window of the room which is just off the kitchen. The tone of Mom's voice was the kind she always used when she was talking to somebody special, the most important person in the world —the One who made the world in the first place, and all the cardinals and other birds and everything in nature.

Just to show you what a wonderful mother I really have, I'll quote part of what she said.

"Thank You, heavenly Father, for sending the cardinal just when You did. I was so upset and angry. I didn't want to be, but I couldn't help it. With all the excitement at the table, I guess I forgot You were still on the throne."

Mom's voice choked then, and it seemed like all the world was still, *so* still I could have heard a caterpillar crawling on a cabbage leaf. Then the cardinal whistled again. This time he was on the other side of the house.

Mom was right. The One who had made the world was still running it. It felt good to be alive.

Looking down into the rain barrel, seeing my face reflected in its yellowish-brown water, I felt extra fine inside. I was remembering another song my parents had taught me when I was little enough to like a song like that. I still thought it was kind of nice, and Charlotte Ann liked it extra well. I could sometimes put her to sleep with it. Sometimes she even tried to sing it herself, having a hard time to pronounce the words, making them sound like:

> One there lived si' by si',
> Two litta maids,
> Each one drest just alike,
> Hair down in braids;
> Blue gingum pin'nfores,
> 'Tockings o' red;
> Litta sunbonnets tied
> On each pitty head.

It was what Mom called a "story song." The second verse tells how the two little maids who lived side by side were angry at each other, and one of them said, "You can't play in my yard!"

But the other said:

> I don't *want* to play in your yard.
> I don't like you any more;
> You'll be sorry when you see me
> Sliding down my cellar door;
> You can't holler down my rain barrel,
> You can't climb my apple tree;
> I don't want to play in your yard,
> If you won't be good to me.

The song was as cute as Charlotte Ann herself—when she was cute, which was quite often, even at the dinner table.

While I was humming the song, there by the rain barrel, I heard myself saying to myself, "Those two girls certainly didn't act very sociable," which they didn't in the first part of the song.

There was another stanza, though, that told about how, the very next day, they were lonesome for each other, and were sorry about their quarrel, so they made up and were good friends all the rest of their lives.

My thoughts were interrupted then by Dad's voice booming from somewhere in the house, coming through the room where Mom was and out the window to where I was by the rain barrel. "There's somebody coming in at the front gate!"

My heart leaped with a different glad feeling. I was almost sure whoever was at the front gate would be one of the gang. I swung away from the rain barrel, swished toward the grape arbor in a hurry to get past it and over the boardwalk, and across the grassy yard to see whichever one of the gang it would be.

My wild dash turned about thirty-seven hens into an excited scatteraway, as if they thought the end of the world had come and they had better fly for their lives.

At the two-foot-high washstand Dad had put beside the boardwalk so we could wash our face and hands outdoors if we wanted to—or if Mom wanted us to—I stopped dead still. Somebody on crutches was hobbling across the yard toward the ivy-shaded side porch, and it was the old black man himself, the tenant who was living in our tree house.

I was surprised to see Mr. Robinson using crutches, when yesterday he had had only a cane.

I hadn't noticed any crutches around the place—but then of course, he could have had them there somewhere. That wasn't what *really* surprised me, though. The thing that absolutely astonished me was that he had only *one leg!* Yesterday he had had *two!* Where his left leg should have been, there was only an empty trouser leg, pinned up with a safety pin, fastened about halfway between where his knee *would* have been, and his hip.

He kept right on coming across the yard, passing the plum tree, where the robin parents had their nest and where right that minute they were scolding like everything because somebody was trespassing on their territory.

When he reached the ivy-shaded porch, I noticed that he was wearing an earphone which he hadn't had on yesterday.

It seemed the old man saw me then for the first time, as, panting for breath, he focused his eyes on me and asked politely, "Are your parents home?"

I could hardly hear his question for wondering what had become of his other leg.

Mom came to the side door then, and I noticed she had found fast time somewhere to straighten her hair a little.

The old man steadied himself with his crutches, smiled a friendly smile, took a deep breath of the hot afternoon air, and said with a tired sigh, "It's such a warm day. But it's cooler down by the creek."

Before Mom could say a word, I heard my voice explode a question at the old man, my curiosity right that minute being the kind that could have killed a wildcat, it was so strong: "How come you got only one leg, when yesterday you had two?"

"Only one leg?" The old man looked down at the short trouser leg, and answered me, "I have an artificial limb. I take it off once in a while to rest my stump. I lost my flesh-and-blood leg years ago in a fight with a lion."

I must have been staring with a wide-open mouth, for he added in explanation, "When I was big-game hunting in Africa." Then as if losing a leg in a fight with a lion wasn't anything worth talking about, he changed the subject and asked, "Do you folks have a tape measure I may borrow? A fifty- or hundred-foot one? I'll bring it back later this afternoon."

Dad was at the door then, too, and so was Charlotte Ann, half hiding between her parents, clinging to Mom's blue, flower-bordered apron.

Mr. Robinson noticed Charlotte Ann, then, and his face lit up with a very friendly smile as he said, "Such a pretty baby!" He shook his head and repeated it, "Such a *pretty* baby!" Then he sort of mumbled something to himself, but which I heard, and it was, "Olive plants. Children are like olive plants around the table." It was an expression used in the Bible about children.

Mom asked the old stranger if he had had any dinner, and he hadn't; and right away she was busy dishing up a plate of roast beef and potatoes and gravy and other things we had left over from dinner.

"Thank you so kindly, Ma'am," Ben Robinson said courteously when Mom invited him to come in and eat at the table, "but I'd like to sit out here under this vine, if I may. It's so friendly and so cool."

I was surprised that, before he ate, the old man bowed his head and closed his eyes, keeping them closed while his lips moved silently. It seemed like maybe God was there in a special way.

The old stranger was taking his last bite of a piece of Mom's apple pie, when from somewhere around the place there came the fiery-red whistle of the cardinal again, calling "Cheer! Cheer! Cheer! or, "Peace! Peace! Peace!" depending on what whoever heard him, was thinking about.

Mom's silver fork on its way to the old man's mouth, stopped; his head jerked up, and his eyes searched the top of the walnut tree and the plum tree and the other trees across the road in the woods.

"Beautiful! *Beautiful*!" he exclaimed, and kept on looking and listening.

The old stranger's last bite of pie was gone when my mind came back to our circle. He finished his cup of coffee, said, "No, thank you," to Mom when she offered him a second cup, then added, "One is just right for my heart. I have to watch it pretty carefully."

He struggled to his feet, with Dad's help.

The old man was puffing hard by the time he was ready to go. I thought of his whiskey flask which he kept water in, looked at his hip pocket to see if it was there, and it was. He started to hobble off across the yard, when Dad ordered me, "Bill, you run out to the toolshed for the tape measure he wanted to borrow."

The old man seemed not to have heard, so I called out to him, "Wait, Mr. Robinson!"

A small jiffy later, when I handed him the tape measure, he said, "Thank you, son. You're a thoughtful boy!" He probably hadn't heard Dad order me to do what I had just done. "I'll bring it back to you later. I just wanted to measure something."

And *that* was our family's introduction to one of the most unusual persons that had ever come to Sugar Creek. If only we had known *who* he was!

I found out more about him that afternoon—*a whole lot more!*

5

BEING CALLED a thoughtful boy, made me want to do something that really was thoughtful, so I walked along kind of half behind and half beside the old man, let him through the front gate, closed the gate thoughtfully, and stayed with him till he had crossed the road and had worked his way through the rail fence—with me helping a little.

He was pretty spry for an old man, even though he was short of breath and had to slow down because of it.

Being extra curious about why he wanted our tape measure, I offered, "I'd be glad to help you measure anything, if you like, Mr. Robinson."

"That's kind of you," he puffed as we moved along, "but I won't need any more help."

I didn't know what he meant by *more* help until quite a while later—quite a long while, in fact. I'll tell you about it when we get that far in the story.

What *did* he want the tape measure for?

I walked all the way down to the creek with him and carried him a pail of fresh water from the spring. I was very careful to look around a little before I left, to see if I could see anything he would need such a long tape measure for, and there wasn't a thing. I decided not to ask him what. He might think it wasn't any of my business.

Back to the house again, I made a beeline for the stack of discouraged dishes and started wiping them —after Mom offered me a chance to do it. For a joke, I said to her, "You certainly are a thoughtful mother. It would have taken you a long time to do them all by yourself."

I didn't exactly want to be thoughtful all afternoon, though, so I said, "After I get through raking the yard,"—Dad had ordered me to do it after I'd finished the dishes—"may I go down to the spring and get you a fresh jug of water?" I was still curious about why the old gentleman had wanted our tape measure.

"As soon as the yard is raked—yes," Mom said, then added, "I wonder how *old* Mr. Robinson is."

Dad, who just then came in the side door, said, "Old enough to have been born away back in the time of Abraham Lincoln." He looked down at me and asked, "You about ready to start on the lawn?"

* * *

"Rake, rake, rake, on thy hot green grass—oh me!" I said to myself, making a parody on the poem in our sixth grade reader that goes, "Break, break, break on thy cold gray stones, O sea!"

In my mind, I was sitting in the cool shade on the log just a few feet from the creek at the best fishing place there is in the daytime. I was watching the different species of dragonflies flitting around my bobber.

I'd been studying dragonflies that summer, as well

as birds. There certainly were a lot of different kinds. Poetry had started a collection of them and already had about ten different-colored, different-shaped, queer-looking specimens. One of the most interesting things I had learned about them was that dragonflies eat thousands of mosquitoes. The adult dragonflies catch the adult mosquitoes in the air; and the dragonfly children, while they are still nymphs living in the water, gobble up the baby mosquitoes living in the same water.

Remembering that there are nearly always a dozen or more baby mosquitoes still in their wriggling stage, swimming around in our rain barrel, I carried my rake over to the corner of the house, where I rested a little by leaning on its long, strong handle. Looking into the yellowish-brown water, I saw my reflection and yelled down at me, "You can't holler down my rain barrel! You can't climb my apple tree! I don't want to play in your yard, if you won't be good to me!"

It's a good thing I did rake the yard, though, because while I was doing it, I accidentally found Poetry's compass out by the orchard fence. Finding it, gave Mom a chance to show what a thoughtful person she was, when she sent me over to Poetry's house to give it to him, having forgotten she wanted me to go to the spring to get a jug of water for her.

When I got to Poetry's toolshed, under which a mother skunk once raised her family of black-and-white little stinkers, I was startled to hear a voice behind me calling, "Hey! Wait for me!"

It was Dragonfly himself, panting and running, like he had something very important on his mind.

Poetry, hearing Dragonfly's yelling, came out from behind the toolshed where he had been, carrying a spade, a tin can, and a cane fishing pole.

" 'Smatter?" I asked Dragonfly.

His answer came out in short, jerky sentences, as he stammered, "Th-th-that old black man! He-he-he's up there in our cemetery measuring things! He's hobbling along from one tombstone to another, and —and—and he's driving stakes and tying white rags on 'em. He-he-he's *trespassing!*"

I was still unhappy in my mind toward Dragonfly on account of his parents having two vacancies at the Green Corn the night before, and there hadn't been even one room for the old man to stay in, so I answered him, "That old cemetery belongs to *everybody*, not to just us. What you so het up about?"

"B-b-but wh-wh-what's he doing with a tape measure measuring all around everywhere?"

The question was one I myself would like the answer to. I hated to help Dragonfly feel any meaner toward the kind old man, so I answered him, "It's my dad's tape measure. He borrowed it from us. Let him measure anything he wants to with it. Who cares?"

"Let's go up and spy on him anyway," Dragonfly said. "See if we c'n see what he's doing in our cemetery."

Poetry disagreed. "That's not *our* cemetery. It belongs to the people who live there and to everybody else. It's the old man's business what he's doing there, anyway.

"Let's go up and offer to help him, if he needs help. That'd be more sociable," I suggested, realizing kind of proudly that I was using one of "Aunt Miriam's" most important words.

"Let's go down to the spring first and get a drink," Poetry suggested, and when I agreed, Dragonfly all of a sudden, exclaimed, "I got to get home. My mother doesn't know where I am."

Without saying anything else, but with a worried look in his eyes, he glanced down at his wristwatch, turned, and started running in the direction of the Gilberts' house.

"What's the matter with that guy?" I asked Poetry. "What makes him so mean in his heart against that innocent old man?"

As soon as Dragonfly was out of sight, Poetry and I started toward the spring which was also toward our tree house; he was carrying his pole and can of worms and the compass I'd given him, and I had my binoculars, so I could watch for birds of different kinds.

"Wait a minute," Poetry said, "I need my butterfly net." When I asked him, "What for?" he answered, "I want to see if I can get another dragonfly for my collection."

"A human one or an insect?" I asked as he left his pole and can of worms and went back into the tool shed.

He answered me over his chubby shoulder, "I know a boy who is both."

It wasn't a very nice thing to say about Dragonfly, and it didn't feel good to have to think it. It was kind of like having a sore finger, to have one of our own gang be the way he was, like Dragonfly wasn't even one of us anymore.

Poetry and I stopped at the Black Widow stump in the open space not far from the linden tree, where we could look up the creek and see our tree house. The sun was pouring its yellow light down on everything; the bees were droning in the creamy yellow flowers of the linden tree. It was the kind of day that made a boy want to be lazy and content to be alive. It seemed like all the animals and birds and everything in nature had a clean heart, because the One who had made the world loved everybody. Part of Dad's prayer came into my mind then, and I remembered he had said, "Give us a greater love for Your Son, our Saviour, for each other and for people of every race and color."

Pretty soon Poetry and I rambled across the sunny space between the stump and the leaning linden tree which grows at the rim of the ridge overlooking the spring. Our getting there scared the afternoon daylights out of a green heron that had been hunting frogs or insects or some other kind of food, and it took off in a long-necked flight straight up the creek in the direction of our weaverbird hideout.

We went on down the slope to the spring itself, where two streams of water tumbled out of two lead pipes into the big cement pool Dad had built there. The lead pipes themselves had been put there several years before when we decided to do what Dad called, "salvage the water," that was coming out in two places from between the layers of sandstone.

The pipes had been driven back into the wall about five feet apart, but the spring water from both of them splashed with a friendly gurgling sound into the same deep, wide pool.

Seeing and hearing the water made me thirsty. In another minute I'd be down on my knees, drinking like a cow out of the pool itself, or else I might decide to use one of the cups from our paper cup dispenser we'd put there for people to use—people like strangers or girls who maybe wouldn't want to drink like a boy. Or if I wanted to, I could hang my head under the end of one of the pipes and drink that way.

And then is when I got the surprise of my life, just as Poetry at the same time let out a whistle that seemed to say, "What on earth!"

There in front of my wondering eyes, standing on the ledge above the first lead pipe, was a foot-square sign that said White, and another sign the same size above the other pipe, that said Colored!

I stood and stared, not wanting to believe my eyes. My thoughts flew up to the cemetery where the old man probably still was. I wondered if he had seen the signs, and what he had felt in his heart about them.

Poetry was the first one of us to find his voice, when he said "Who on earth would do a thing like that! We don't have signs like that in America anymore! Not in Sugar Creek territory, anyway!"

"You suppose maybe Dragonfly—"

"Don't say it—don't even *think* it!" Poetry exclaimed. "It'd almost *have* to be an older person who used to live in some part of America where they *did* have signs like that on drinking fountains and on doors to restaurants. But there's *not* anybody *we* know who would do it."

"Sh! Listen," Poetry exclaimed under his breath. "Somebody's coming!"

We scurried for the board fence in the direction of the swimming hole, squeezed through, and hid ourselves behind the underbrush there.

"It's the old man, himself," Poetry who saw him first, said. I noticed that he had his artificial leg on again and that he hardly limped at all, as he worked his way down, using only his cane to steady himself. Also he was half singing and half humming a song we had sung a few times in school during Opening Exercises. It is in the book name, *One Hundred and One Best Songs* and is called, "Swing Low, Sweet Chariot."

Reaching the bottom of the incline, Mr. Robinson stopped beside the reservoir, and took his flask from his hip pocket.

He stopped singing then and peered at the two signs we boys had seen a few minutes before.

The old man's head dropped forward like I had seen it do at our house before he had started to eat what Mom had given him, and I heard him say as clear as anything, "That's all right, Lord. They probably don't know why they do it."

Right away, the old man was singing again, a little louder than before, I thought, beginning right where he had left off, the place being:

> A band of angels, comin' after me,
> Comin' for to carry me Home.

I was wondering as I was crouching there with Poetry behind the underbrush, how long it would be before a band of angels would actually come to carry him to heaven. I hoped it wouldn't be soon.

My thoughts came back just in time to see Mr. Robinson fill his flask from the water that came tumbling out of the pipe that said Colored above it; then he took a pill from the small bottle in his pocket, put it to his mouth, took a swallow of water from the flask, filled the flask again, and started back up the incline, walking slowly and very carefully and puffing a little from being short of breath.

Not till we were sure the old man was beyond hearing us, did either of us say a word to each other. Poetry spoke first. "Of course Dragonfly *could* have done it!"

Then we heard footsteps again, not slow and faltering steps like the old man's had been, but those of somebody running; in fact, it sounded like the steps of quite a few people.

Poetry and I dropped back into our hiding place, getting there just as down the leaf-strewn incline trotted Old Bawler, one of Circus' dad's hounds. With his long ears flapping and his long tongue hanging out, he went straight to the reservoir, sniffed around like he was wondering something or other, then lifted his head with its sad face, and looked back up the incline just as Circus reach the brink.

Bawler was what is called a "black and tan," and his voice when crying on a coon trail was the most beautiful night sound anybody ever heard, like a cornet part of the time, and like an organ's highest tones the rest of the time.

Before Circus started down, Old Bawler dropped his sad-faced head to the pool of fresh, cool water and began to lap it up with his tongue.

"He shouldn't drink out of it like that," Poetry whispered sarcastically in my ear. "Some dog of some other color might have taken a drink there this morning, and he might get some kind of dog contamination," he said, using an extra long word like he sometimes does, his family having a dictionary at their house too.

The second Circus reached the bottom of the slope, I saw his body stiffen. His eyes were looking at the two signs like they were burning holes in them. Then as if he had made up his mind to do the same thing I'd had in mind to do, he stepped across the reservoir to the other side. I was sure he was going to tear those signs to pieces.

But he didn't. Instead, he took a cup from the dispenser, held it under the end of the pipe that had the Colored sign, let it fill all the way up, lifted it to his lips, and drank. He sighed then, shook his head, folded the cup, and tucked it into his shirt pocket, and called, "Here, Bawler! Come here!"

Bawler, who had already come over to the fence

we were hiding behind, sniffing suspiciously in our direction, left us and went back to his master.

Then Circus reached for the sign that said White, and let Bawler sniff it, as he asked, "You know anybody who would put up a sign like that?"

Bawler looked up, let out a friendly little chop that seemed to say, "Sorry, but I wouldn't know."

"Take a good smell," Circus ordered him, "and if you ever smell the hands of anybody who might have left his scent on this card, let me know." He put the sign back where it had been.

Bawler took a few quick laps of water from the reservoir, licked his chops, looked up again as if to say, "It wouldn't be any dog *I* know." Then he and Circus took off up the slope and disappeared over the ridge.

As soon as we knew we were alone, Poetry asked me, "Did you notice what I noticed?"

"What?" I asked; and he told me, "He took his drink out of the Colored side, instead of out of the White."

"Listen!" I whispered an exclamation.

We listened, and it was Circus' high soprano voice coming from somewhere up near the Black Widow stump, singing, "Swing low, Sweet chariot—"

A happy feeling welled up in my heart for good old monkey-faced, beautiful-voiced, dark-haired, Circus Brown, one of the best boys in the whole Sugar Creek territory and maybe in the whole world.

I had further reason to be proud of Circus before the afternoon was over.

6

CIRCUS' MELODIOUS VOICE singing the old Negro spiritual hadn't any sooner faded away into the woods, than Poetry suggested with a command in his voice, "Let's hurry up and take the old man his can of worms before he starts his afternoon nap. We'll probably find him at the Sociable Weaverbird Motel."

It sounded strange to hear our grass-roofed tree house called that. It also sounded fine and made me feel proud. I was also proud of Poetry; Mom would be proud of him, too, when she found out about his digging the can of worms for the old man. Mom especially liked people of some other race or color, and every Sunday she would put an extra offering in her church envelope for missions. The very next time Poetry accidentally stopped at our house on baking day to get his usual small piece of pie, Mom would give him an extra large slice.

Right away we were on our way, Poetry whistling a tune of some kind, and I whistling the same one in my mind.

In only a few moseying minutes, we were at the tree house. Like the gang made it a rule to do when we were near anybody's camping place—since it isn't good manners to walk right into anybody's privacy—Poetry called, "Anybody home? Hello!"

When there was no answer, and the old gentleman wasn't anywhere in sight, we decided to go on up to the cemetery to see if he was there.

We skirted the border of the bayou, climbed over the rail fence into the Gilberts' cornfield, followed the hedgerow to the bottom of Bumblebee Hill, working our way toward the top, through the thick shrubbery that grew along the steep slope. The gang hardly ever went that way on account of there were a lot of stones and briers there.

Pretty soon, with my curiosity still tingling to see what we would see when we got to the top and why the old gentleman was using our tape measure, we finally reached the crest, where the shrubbery was the densest and the blackberry vines the thickest, and also where the stone fence began. There we stopped to catch our breath and to look and listen.

I guess Poetry and I both heard voices at the same time; the wind was blowing toward us, so it was easier for us to hear whoever was over in the cemetery than it would be for anybody there to hear us.

I said we both heard *voices*—the old man's voice, and a boy's voice answering. They seemed to be coming nearer, in fact, right toward our hiding place which was behind the stone fence not far from Old Man Paddler's wife's gravestone—the tall one that has the chiseled hand on it with one finger pointing toward the sky, and the words that say, "There is rest in heaven."

Poetry and I kept each other shushed with our eyes and with our forefingers to our lips. I was all ears to hear what I felt pretty sure was going to be something very important.

"It's very kind of you," the old gentleman said. "He's such a beautiful hound, and there's nothing I'd like better than to go racing along the creek at night listening to the hounds in full cry on a coon or fox trail. But my old joints won't stand it anymore. I haven't done it for years—not since I left for Africa the last time. Hunting there was an entirely different kind."

Circus' beginning-to-change voice, asked, "Did you kill any aardvarks?"

Before Mr. Robinson's answer, my mind flew up to the alcove in our upstairs, and I was looking at "Miriam's" very first page, seeing a picture of a long-eared, long-nosed, ridiculous-looking animal which "Miriam" says lives on nothing but ants, which it burrows through the ground to catch with its long slimy tongue.

"No aardvarks, but I *saw* quite a number. You boys must let me tell you some of our safari experiences some time. What's your hound's name?"

"Bawler. Bawler Brown," Circus Brown answered.

I peeped through a crack in the stone fence just in time to see Bawler's long nose sniff at Mr. Robinson's outstretched hand and lick it like a dog does when he likes you.

Another thing Circus suggested right then was, "Bawler's a good watchdog, too, if you'd like him to stay with you some night. He's a fierce fighter. You wouldn't have to be afraid if he was sleeping outside your door."

I was having a hard time keeping quiet, but when I heard the next four or five minutes of what Circus and the old man said to each other, I was certainly glad I did. Maybe I can't quote it exactly like they said it, but this is most of it, anyway.

Circus said first, "I don't know who put those signs down at the spring, but if it was any of our gang, whichever one it was, he's going to get some pretty rough treatment from the rest of us."

"Don't do it, son," the old stranger said firmly, and repeated, "Don't do it. I lived much of my early life where there were signs like that in many public places—on drinking fountains, in bus and train depots, hotels—and even some restaurants didn't like to serve people of other races. I confess I was surprised to find prejudice like that in this part of our country. But a man shouldn't spoil his mind by feeding it on resentments. Life is too short for that. I've given my heart over to winning souls to Christ."

For a few minutes, while I crouched there beside Poetry, I could hardly see for some crazy old tears getting into my eyes. A lump of love or something came into my throat and in my mind I was back in our one-room school again, hearing Miss Trillium say, "All human beings are the handwriting of God. He uses different colored inks."

But Circus wasn't satisfied, "I still feel it's an insult."

"I know," the kind voice of the old man answered. "It may have been intended for that, but I refuse to accept it as such. After all, the sin, if that's what it is, is in the mind of the *other* person, don't you think? I am so glad that the love of Christ is working to change people. We're all human beings, and I am sure the time will come when we will find a way to live and work together in a friendly manner. Let's give each other a little more time. The Bible says "He that hates his brother is a murderer."

When the old man said that, it was like I had been stabbed in the heart, on account of I was still so angry at Dragonfly. It's a strange feeling—loving and hating the same person at the same time.

"Even in nature," the old gentleman went on, "the blackbirds flock together—and the sparrows and bluebirds and wild geese. They get along in the same woods, and they don't spend all their time fighting each other.

"Take that tree house you've rented me. I've seen the real thing in Africa. Hundreds of pairs of weaverbirds living in the same big, umbrella-shaped nest. No other birds of any other species dared try to make their home with them. There would have been bird war—though as we all know, sometimes birds even of the same species, fight each other, and one swarm of bees will attack and rob another hive of their honey.

"That's the way it is in nature. But we are God's *highest* creatures. We have souls, and we ought to love one another. The Bible says, "*Be ye kind one to another, tenderhearted, forgiving one another, even as God for Christ's sake hath forgiven you."*

The old man's tone of voice changed then. It was as if Circus wasn't there, but a big crowd of people instead, and he was making a speech as he went on.

"Here in America, we have our misunderstandings, but it's a good country. I am proud to be an American, proud also that I belong to the black race. During the Civil War, of the one million-five hundred thousand men who fought for the Union, two-hundred-thirty thousand were Negroes—the thirty thousand fighting in the navy. My own father was killed in the Battle of Bull Run.

"There are over fifteen million of us living in America today, and included in our number are successful people of all professions and occupations, and of both high and low social standing.

"Some of the world's greatest athletes are Negroes, even Olympic champions. Some of our people are bad people, which is true also of every race, but many of us are serving the Lord and doing His will —true also of every race."

It was easy to listen to, although it was kind of hard to hear every word. After two or three minutes of talking like he was making a speech, the old man's voice changed back to its gentle, quavering tone, and he was talking to Circus again, finishing. "Yes, I am thankful and proud to be black."

He stopped altogether, and I could actually hear him breathing—in fact, kind of heavily, like he had been running in a race or climbing a hill fast.

Then Circus said something that gave me the

surprise of my life. You could have knocked me over with a breath of fresh air, I was so astonished when he said, "Mr. Robinson, I'm not only proud to be an American but I'm also proud to have *Indian* blood in my veins. My great-great-grandmother on my father's side was half Indian. Nobody around here knows it because our family moved here from Missouri fifty years ago. Even my folks don't know *I* know it, but I read it in an old diary I found in the bottom of a trunk in the attic," Circus finished with a proud voice.

Mr. Robinson's answer made me feel fine, when he said, "Don't ever be ashamed of it, son. Always remember that Indians were the very first Americans."

And Circus answered, "Maybe that's why I like hunting and fishing so well, and everything in nature. Maybe I inherited it."

Right that second, Bawler, who had been lying at the old man's feet, raised his head like he was proud to be a dog, and pointed a suspicious nose in the direction of the other side of the cemetery, which is the direction the wind was still coming from. He was on his four feet a jiffy later, his nose still suspicious. Then he growled an unfriendly growl as much as to say, "I don't like whoever's over there."

" 'Smatter, Bawler?" Circus asked, and Bawler answered with a deep-voiced, growling chop, with his nose still in the direction of the other side of the cemetery. He stood stiff-legged with the hair on his back bristling—which is what a dog's hair on his back always does when his temper is bristling on the *inside* of him.

"See what a good watchdog he is?" Circus asked. "If you'd just let him stay with you tonight, he'd tear anybody to pieces who tried to break in and take any of your money or hurt you. There are some mean men over in Halifax County, who resent black people, Mr. Robinson. They burned a cross at Sam Ballard's the other night. If anybody tried to do that in front of *your* house, Bawler'd stop him if he was your watchdog, wouldn't you, Bawler?"

Bawler heard his name, growled a friendly little chop as much as to say that whoever was on the other side of the cemetery wasn't important or dangerous anyway, turned back, licked Circus' outstretched hand, and lay down again at the old man's feet. I noticed, though, that he still kept his eyes and ears and nose pointed toward the direction from which the wind was blowing.

Bawler hadn't any sooner settled down than he had to get up again, because Circus decided it was time for him to go. I noticed that Bawler was still suspicious as he sort of led the way for Circus in the path that winds to the north side of the cemetery and on down across the battleground of the battle of Bumblebee Hill.

No sooner was Circus out of sight than the old gentleman began talking again.

"He's praying," Poetry whispered.

I knew the words weren't meant for any human being to hear. I couldn't hear them very well, anyway—only a few mumbled phrases about being tired and short of breath. Part of one sentence came through clear though, and was: "I don't know why You let *me* live instead of him, when I've done so little with my life."

That was all I could hear. In fact, the old gentleman stopped talking after that and yawned, stretched like he was sleepy, then did the strangest thing. He pulled his right trouser leg up to and above his knee, unstrapped his artificial limb, and took it off.

If only I could have whispered to Poetry without being heard by Mr. Robinson, I'd have said, "Look how red and inflamed his stump is. No wonder he takes his leg off now and then and uses crutches."

After the leg was off, Benjamin Robinson took off his earphone and tucked it into his shirt pocket—maybe to give his ear a rest too.

Poetry and I knew then that we could whisper to each other. The very first thing he said to me was, "He's got a map."

I watched with my heart pounding in my ears, wondering what was going on in the old man's mind. After he had studied the map a while—if it was a map—he yawned, stretched, wormed his way over to the deeper shade of the pine tree near Sarah Paddler's tombstone, leaving his artificial limb lying in the sun. Making a pillow out of his light coat, he lay down, closed his eyes and in only a few jiffies, was breathing heavily and regularly, meaning he probably was asleep.

It was what Mom would call a peaceful scene. The breeze was rippling the bluegrass around the gravestones, stirring the leaves of the sweetbrier bushes and making the tall straight mullein stalks swagger like drunk men trying to walk. If there hadn't been so much on my mind, it would have been a good time to take an afternoon nap. But I wasn't sleepy. In fact, I was very wide awake a second later when I saw something glittering in the grass; it was the metal case of Dad's new tape measure.

We had come up to see the old man and to find out what he was measuring, also to give him a can of worms, and he had gone to sleep on us.

"Let's go see if we can find out what Old Bawler was suspicious about," I suggested to Poetry. "Maybe it was Dragonfly."

"It better not be," Poetry said grimly, and I could feel his temper bristling. Both our tempers were hot, and as we moved along the trail Circus had followed, our minds like Old Bawler's nose were pointing toward every direction to see if we could see anything out of the ordinary. *Somebody* had put the signs at the spring. Somebody who didn't like black people and maybe didn't like the members of the Sugar Creek Gang, unless it was Dragonfly who was *supposed* to like us.

"Circus Brown's a pretty nice guy," Poetry said to me, puffing, as we rambled along, stopping every now and then to peek through my binoculars, or to untangle his butterfly net from a brier or bush it got caught on.

"Pretty nice, is right," I answered.

At the foot of Bumblebee Hill, we circled the Little Jim Tree, scouted our way down toward the

Black Widow stump again, all the time keeping our eyes peeled to see if we could see what had made old Bawler so suspicious.

"Maybe we'll run into Circus down here somewhere," one of us said to the other—I can't remember which—and neither of us answered a word.

When we were getting near our tree house, Poetry suggested, "Let's leave our can of worms and a note just outside the door so he'll know what they're for."

But we didn't leave our can of worms, and we *didn't* leave any note. The reason we didn't was because there was a note already there—not written with pencil or pen but *printed* in large letters on a placard the same size as the cards at the spring, one of which, you remember, said Colored and the other White.

My temper came to the hottest life it had come to in a long time when we reached the edge of the clearing and saw on the seat of the captain's chair we had put there for the old man to use, and propped up against the chair's back, the foot-square white placard, and on it the words:

White Only

Not only that, but the ashes from the fireplace we'd built for the old man, were scattered all over, the pail of water I'd carried earlier in the afternoon was spilled on the ground, with the pail itself lying on its side just inside the tree house door!

7

POETRY AND I stood frozen in our tracks at what some unsociable person had done—practically ordering our tenant out of *our* house! Imagine *that*!

My imagination kept seeing Old Bawler standing stiff-legged with his nose pointed in this direction, and I wished I could know with my mind what I knew his nose knew.

My eyes were still focused on the insulting words on the placard, when my ears caught the sound of something going on farther up the bayou.

"Sounds like somebody digging," I whispered. "*Kerslup—scrish—kerslup—scrish—*" It was like a shovel or spade being filled with dirt and emptied. *Filled—emptied—filled—emptied.*

Then the digging seemed to stop, and we heard an entirely different sound, like somebody chopping with an ax or hatchet.

"Let's find out what's going on *right now*!" Poetry whispered.

I looked into his set face to see if he meant it, and he did.

Like my heart always does at a time like that, it was pounding in my ears, and I was feeling pretty tense as we carefully picked our way through the underbrush toward the sound of the chopping ax or hatchet. I just knew that when we got there, we'd see some strange person, maybe someone with a fierce face and powerful muscles and an explosive temper who—

But that was as far as my thoughts went, because Poetry let out a surprised "It's only Little Jim, digging!"

Right away we were both where Little Jim was. He had quite a good-sized hole dug at the base of a small tree.

"What you digging sassafras roots for?" Poetry demanded, squinting up at the only tree that grows around Sugar Creek which has three different kinds of leaves on the same twig, the three kinds being what our schoolteacher calls, "oval," "two-lobed," and "three-lobed."

Little Jim answered Poetry with a mouse-like squeak in his small voice, "For Mr. Robinson, so he can have sassafras tea."

For a second, a discouraging idea came into my mind. It was: Poetry dug a can of worms for our tenant; Circus offered his hound for a watchdog; Little Jim dug sassafras roots so he can make some of the best-tasting tea there ever was; and I, Bill Collins, haven't planned to do a single thing for him! All I had done was to go to our toolshed to get Dad's tape measure for him, he having asked for it first. Of course, I'd helped him through the rail fence across from our mailbox, and had carried a pail of water for him, but what I'd done didn't seem important.

My mind came back to our little circle of things when Poetry said to me, "Little Jim's got his bird guide with him."

There wasn't anything unusual about that, on account of that summer he carried it around with him nearly all the time. He was as proud as I was about what he knew about different kinds of birds, especially since I had told him that all the birds in the world were divided into two classes: *altricial* and *precocial*. Over and over and over, the past several weeks, he had been using the words, saying them to himself, and whenever he'd see a bird, he'd call out its name and what kind it was. He almost wore those two long words out from using them so much.

Right while he was yanking at a piece of sassafras root he was trying to pry loose, he stopped, looked up and all around, listened in several directions, holding one small hand up to his ear, and exclaimed, "Hear that! It's going to rain!"

I'd heard it myself, a rain crow spouting off with a long-drawn-out series of "kuks," sounding like "kuk-kuk-kuk-kuk-kuk-kuk" in a harsh, grating voice from up in some tree along the bayou.

"I've got to *see* him!" Little Jim cried. Looking at his wristwatch to see what time it was, he dropped his shovel and started off with his bird guide on a fast, short-legged run toward the bayou.

A very few seconds later, I heard Little Jim yell back to us from the rail fence that borders the bayou, "I see him. He's a yellow-billed *altricial* cuckoo! Com'ere quick!"

The "rain crow" and the "yellow-billed cuckoo"

were different names for the same bird. Because it did more "kuk-kuk-kuk-kuk"-ing in rainy weather, many people around Sugar Creek thought it was a very good weather prophet.

About that same second, an actual flying dragonfly came gliding into where we were, darting here and there, looking like a small four-winged airplane. When Poetry saw it, he mimicked Little Jim's excitement and cried, "Look! There goes a *devil's darning needle!*"

And Poetry was right. The speeding dragonfly was an actual *green darner*, which is its true name.

Poetry, as if he had forgotten all about the insulting sign practically ordering the old man to pack up and get out, started on a fast chase after the *green darner*, swinging his butterfly net and panting and dodging all over the place.

We were almost a hundred yards from our homemade boys' nest, when we woke up to the fact that we had lost a lot of time. We turned around and hurried back, and found the old man standing about ten feet from the entrance, steadying himself with his cane, reading the sign.

What to do! What can you do when there isn't a thing you can think of *to* do?

You feel all of a sad sudden that you want to run over to the old gentleman, tottering on his cane, look into his eyes, and exclaim to him, "Don't you worry, Mr. Robinson! Don't you worry one little bit! The Sugar Creek Gang'll never stand for a thing like that! We're American citizens in the land of the free and the home of the brave, and we're not going to stand for anybody robbing any of our citizens of their freedom!"

Then my muscles leaped into the fight my mind was already in the middle of. I dashed across the space between myself and the placard with the insulting words on it, grabbed it up, and tore it to pieces, dashed the pieces onto the ground, and stamped my feet on them. I was still stamping on them, when there was a streak of small boy flying across the open space to where I was—and Little Jim was there, too, stamping his own small feet on them right along with my kind of large feet.

"There, Mr. Robinson!" I exclaimed to him proudly. *"That's* what the Sugar Creek Gang thinks of a thing like that! We don't know who put it there, but none of us did."

It certainly felt fine to say what I had said, and even better to *do* what I had *done*.

The old man began to sway dizzily, steadied himself with his cane, staggered to his captain's chair where the sign had been a few jiffies before, looked all around, took a deep breath and said to us; "I've always been proud of my race, boys. We've supplied some of the world's best athletes; some of its greatest inventors; thousands of our soldiers fought and died in both world wars. I haven't lived in our country too much of my life, for when I was a young man I went to Africa as a missionary to help win my ancestors to Christ. That's where I lost my leg—in a fight with a lion when I was hunting big game. I always liked to hunt."

He stopped talking then, heaved a sigh, slumped

to his chair, let out a groan, lowered his voice as if he were going to tell us something very important.

"If you boys can stay a few minutes, there's something I'd like you to know. Right now in some parts of our country there is a lot of bitterness and what is called racism. Another name for it is race hatred. This is not right in God's sight.

"Also, boys, people of different groups are trampling on the hearts of innocent people. If only we could give each other, and God too, a little more time, and love each other the way the Saviour loved us all—"

He stopped, focused his eyes on the scattered pieces of cardboard and said, "I wonder what it would be like to die, come up to heaven's gate, and find a sign on the door: White Only."

For a second or maybe ten or twenty, after the old man said that, everything was very quiet, none of us saying a word. Away over the top of the hill, where I was looking at the time, there was a white cloud hanging in the afternoon sky. From somewhere along the creek behind us a crow let out a worried caw-caw-caw, as if it was lonesome for its mate.

It was Little Jim who answered the old man, and his answer showed what kind of mind he had—and maybe, also, what kind of parents he had—when he said, "If the word 'White' meant 'Pure in heart,' it'd be all right, for the pure in heart get to see God, but if it meant white *skin*, it wouldn't *be* the gate to heaven, for God looks on the kind of hearts people have."

And again everything was quiet, with even nature seeming to agree. Just then a lively—in fact *very* lively—wind swept across the bayou, woke up the leaves in the trees, and the sound they made was a little like a crowd of people clapping their hands—like it says in one of Mom's favorite Bible verses, "And all the trees of the field shall clap their hands."

Right that second I saw a blank expression come over the wrinkled old face. He raised his hand to his forehead, a helpless look came into his eyes, his other hand fumbled in his shirt pocket for the small bottle I'd seen him take from there before. His breath began to come hard and fast; he leaned forward, like first aid rules say to do if you feel faint. He reached in his hip pocket for the flask he kept there, managed to get it out, but there wasn't a drop of water in it—not even a drop.

The old man sank back in his chair, and gasped, "Water! Get me a drink!"

How I ever managed to get to the spring and back with a pail of water, I don't know, but I did, and in time to rescue the old man from his heart attack. When his breathing was normal again, he straightened up in his chair, smiled, and said, "That was pretty close. The worst spell I've had for a long time." He looked the three of us over. "You ready to hear what I want to tell you? You can pass it on to the rest of the boys of your club."

In a little while we were in the midst of listening to one of the strangest, saddest stories I'd heard in my life. I won't take time to write every word of it for you, but this is most of it:

Before Mr. Robinson was born, his parents were slaves way back in American history in the time of Abraham Lincoln. Some slave owners were very kind to their slaves, and others were not, but were like Simon Legree in *Uncle Tom's Cabin.*

One night Ben's parents ran away from their master, hiding in haystacks and barns in the daytime, and fleeing at night, getting farther and farther away from the part of America where they had been living.

"Finally," the old man's trembling voice said, "they reached the Sugar Creek country, and here my mother became very ill. They were afraid to try to get a doctor, and there—*here* somewhere—the climax came, and a baby boy was born—*born dead!*

"About fifteen minutes later, another baby boy was born, and a half hour after that my mother died.

"I was that second baby.

"My father knew he couldn't stay here. He would have to go on or be caught and taken back. He waited till night, went to a farmhouse, borrowed a spade without permission, and somewhere in this area, dug a grave, and buried my mother and my little twin brother. He returned the spade, and taking me with him, hurried on into the North, hoping to reach Canada. But they caught up with us, took us back to the plantation. Then the Civil War broke out, and Father ran away again and joined the Union Army, and was finally killed in the battle of Bull Run.

"Later I was adopted into a Christian family, and

I grew up without knowing anything of all this—not until many years later. My foster parents were very kind to me, giving me a good education in school and in the church. But I kept thinking of my real father and mother, wondering who they were. All I could learn was that they had been slaves, that they had run away from their master, and that both had died when I was very young.

"I might never have known anything of all this if my father hadn't written it all down. Some time ago, after I had finished a series of lectures on my experiences in Africa, a lady in my audience handed me a very old campaign poster with some words and arrows scrawled on the back. Apparently, Father had wanted a record of his wife's death and his son's birth. And he drew a rough map so he might return someday and put up a proper marker on the grave.

"The lady who gave it to me had just that week found it in an old trunk in her grandfather's home. Her grandfather had been a soldier in the Confederate army. In the battle of Bull Run in hand-to-hand fighting, he had killed a Union soldier.

"In his dying moments that soldier had gasped: 'The paper in my pocket! Find my son and give it to him.' "

Benjamin Robinson, sitting sadly in our captain's chair by the door of our weaverbird house, looked like a very tired, very old but wonderful human being, I thought. He wasn't through talking, so he went on. "The poster had a description of what my father called 'the Sugar Creek Territory.'

"I know that *this* is the geographical area he meant; it's the only Sugar Creek country in America that could possibly fit the description."

Again the old stranger stopped, his eyes lighting up for a minute as they followed the flight of a swallowtail butterfly that came floating through the air near where we were, and lighted on a half-rotten apple near the outdoor fireplace. Swallowtails like rotten fruit almost better than they do orange-colored milkweed flowers. "I hope," Mr. Robinson said, "there will be swallow tail butterflies in heaven. I'm afraid I'll miss them if there aren't."

But he let his story be interrupted only a few seconds. Right away he went back to it again. "As soon as I find where my mother and little brother were buried, I'll put up a marker. That's why I'm here."

I could hardly see straight for the tears that all of a sudden were in my eyes. I couldn't help but think, *What if my own wonderful mother were buried in the woods or along the bayou near here, and nobody knew for sure where?*

My sad thoughts were interrupted just then by Little Jim piping up and asking, "What was your little brother's name?"

"Benjamin," was the surprising answer.

"But that's *your* name," Poetry put in.

"That's right. My parents had planned to name their new baby Benjamin, if it was a boy. When he was born dead, they gave the name to me."

I noticed Dad's tape measure lying in the grass beside the captain's chair. "We'll be glad to help you find their grave if you want us to," I offered.

"Thank you, son. You boys are certainly kind to an old man. I'm not sure, but I think I found it this afternoon."

He yawned, his eyes closed, and he stretched like Dad does before he decides he has to take a nap. "I think my new medicine makes me sleepy."

We left the old man lying on the cot we had brought for him and went back to our different homes, wondering just *where* his mother's and little brother's grave was. What kind of marker would he put up? It would seem strange having a tombstone somewhere in the woods. Just where *would* it be? Also, he'd need help to put one up, especially if it was a large stone. Somebody would have to bring it out from town in a wagon or a truck. Would he put up just one, or would there be two?

There was something else I was wondering as I passed "Theodore Collins" on our mailbox and started to go across the road to help Theodore Collins in our barn, finish the chores. What if their grave was on Gilberts' property?

At the supper table, where Charlotte Ann had better baby manners than she had for a long time, Dad astonished me by something he said. "I stopped at the Green Corn on the way home from town. Remember the rainy night when Ben Robinson borrowed your Tree House Motel?"

I remembered, and was beginning to feel unhappy again toward the Gilberts for having turned him away, when Dad explained, "The Gilberts had their No Vacancy sign on because those last two units had been reserved by telephone, but there was a bridge out, and the parties didn't arrive. So, son," Dad stopped and looked at me with an I-told-you-so expression in his eyes; then he finished, "The Gilberts aren't the hard-hearted people you think they are."

Mom sighed and said, "That I'm very glad to hear. I didn't want to believe it."

My father took a sip of coffee, wiped his mustache with his napkin, and really astonished me with, "What I know you'll be surprised to learn is that the Longs are back. They didn't like the climate where they moved, and they've come back to their farm. They've been staying at the Green Corn this week, while their home is being redecorated and modernized."

A bewildered feeling swept into my mind as I realized the peace and quiet of the Sugar Creek territory was going to be interrupted again. My first question was "Are they going to take over the woods again? Will Shorty have his blue cow again?"

A whirlwind of unhappy memories picked me up and sent me spinning through the worried summer we'd spent when the Longs had lived here before. That was maybe the worst summer the gang had ever had, and it was all because of the short, fat Long boy, named Guenther, whose nickname was Shorty.

Shorty had a short temper and used it on almost everything and everybody, especially Theodore Collins' short-tempered son.

Most of our trouble had been caused by Shorty's blue cow, which they had pastured in the woods across the road from our place. Shorty himself had named her *Babe* after the blue ox in the stories of the Northwest lumberjack, Paul Bunyan.

And Babe had been anything but a *baby.* She certainly couldn't be cow-sat with, as I found out one sad morning when she broke into our clover field and stuffed herself with dew-wet ladino clover, swelled up, and scared Mom and me half to death.

But, I thought, as I sat across the table from my father, I *had* saved Babe's life by jabbing a tubelike instrument called a trocar into her paunch.

Shorty Long's meanest action that summer had been to almost break up our gang by turning Dragonfly against the rest of us.

It was what Dad said next that turned on a light in my mind and made me feel all whirlwindy and bothered. "You boys won't need to worry about having trouble with the Long boy this summer. He's calmed down a lot, his father told me. He's developing his talent for painting, and has done some very fine landscapes. Right now he's doing sign-painting—he's especially good at lettering—and hopes to make a little extra money working for the Sugar Creek Art Designers."

What on earth! In fact, *double* what on earth! My mind flew down to the spring and read two signs, very neatly lettered, one of which said, "White" and the other "Colored."

Another sign came into my brain, that had been standing on Ben Robinson's captain's chair, and read "White Only."

There's one other thing you ought to know that

Dad learned at the Green Corn that afternoon. One reason the Longs had moved to Sugar Creek was that the community where they lived for a year was still having race problems, and Guenther was building up some bitter feelings against blacks.

When Dad finished telling us what he'd learned at the Green Corn, I thought I understood Dragonfly a little better, and didn't feel quite so hurt in my heart against him. But I did feel very stubborn against one of the worst boy enemies I'd ever had in all my half-long life—Guenther "Shorty" Long.

That short-tempered, fierce-fighting, mean-minded boy had moved back into our territory again, and already he was causing trouble by painting signs for Dragonfly to put up at the spring and at our tree house, and—I felt sure of it—was making the heart of an old man feel terribly sad.

Mom looked at Dad, sighed and said, "Dragonfly's parents are such fine people, and the Longs, too. I can't understand why Guenther is such a bully—I mean, excuse me for using such a word about a boy who doesn't have any excuse to be that way."

Dad's answer surprised me: "Some boys are born leaders; they seem to *have* to have followers. If they can get the right kind of training, they'll make their mark in the world, and do a lot of good."

"I know," Mom nodded, and added, "but the poor followers—the boys who have wishy-washy hearts, and can't stand on their own two feet!"

And again Dad's answer surprised me, when he said to Mom—neither of them looking in my direction, even though I knew their thoughts *and* their words were meant for me—"*Until* a boy finds out he has two feet to stand on, his parents have to teach him how to walk."

I looked at Charlotte Ann in her chair, and for a flash of a few seconds, thought about how many times she had fallen down while *she* was learning to walk. I'd seen her take a tumble maybe forty times a day—in the kitchen, in the living room, out on the lawn, all over everywhere.

My thoughts came back into our kitchen in time to hear Mom say about Dragonfly's parents, his mother in particular: "Lilly is *such* a sincere person, so tenderhearted. She's trying the best way she knows to bring up her boy in the way he ought to go, like it says in Proverbs, 'Train up a child in the way he should go: and when he is old, he will not depart from it.' I've been watching the family grow these years since the time we all were down on the Mexican border, and they surrendered their lives—" Mom stopped, swallowed like a lump of love or something had come into her throat, and she couldn't finish.

I knew she was remembering a very wonderful night when the Gang had all been down at the bottom of the United States on a winter vacation, and Dragonfly's parents, and mine had been with us as chaperones, and *both* Dragonfly's parents had heard the gospel and had been saved—actually and honestly.

Dragonfly himself, I remembered, had trusted in Christ one day down along the creek when he was coming down a sycamore tree like Zachaeus did in the Bible. But he was still wishy-washy minded and had been easily influenced by Guenther Long.

Mom added one more thing right then, and it was, "I didn't *want* to think they'd have any bitterness toward a person of another race. What's the difference, anyway, what the color of a person's skin is?"

I hadn't planned to put in what I thought of to say right then, but it was out before I knew it. "God has a right to write with any color ink He wants to."

Dad cleared his throat, wiped his mustache with his napkin, took a drink of coffee, and his eyes met Mom's in the same way I'd seen them meet quite a few times when he thought she was a pretty wonderful human being. Then he stood, went to the stove, came back with the coffee pot, and poured Mom and himself another cup.

Charlotte Ann held up her mug, which Dad filled with white milk, and she didn't know the difference.

Then Dad said something that was as good a sermon as I'd ever heard in church, and was, "When Lazarus came out of the grave, he was alive all right, but he was still bound with his graveclothes. The Gilberts are *new* Christians. They have *life*, but like a lot of all of us, they—and we—need to help set each other free from bad habits and unkind feelings that displease the Lord. Also, it just may be that the Longs have never even heard the Saviour's voice calling them to life. We ought to pray for them as well as for ourselves."

When I went up to my room that night, I was remembering what Dad had said about graveclothes, and also remembering the Bible story itself, which before we'd left the table, he had read to us from the eleventh chapter of St. John.

My thoughts got a little mixed up for a while, and I was back in Palestine with the disciples, out in the cemetery where Lazarus was buried. It seemed like the Saviour was standing just outside the open cave, which was the kind of grave it was, and there were hundreds of people watching to see what He would do.

Then the Lord called out with a loud voice, "Lazarus, come forth!"

And out Lazarus came—only there were two boys with him, one a spindle-legged, pop-eyed little guy named Roy Gilbert, and the other a boy named Guenther Long, and both boys were wrapped 'round and 'round with grave wrappings. It seemed like I was supposed to rush up quick and help the disciples unwrap Dragonfly and Shorty.

As I pulled Mom's nice, sweet-smelling sheet up over me, it felt good to be alive, but not to be awake. I'd have to get some sleep. There were a lot of important things to do in the morning.

The very next thing I knew it *was* morning, and ahead of me was a wonderful day. Also, a very exciting and even dangerous one.

Before I tell you about it, I have to tell you first about something very sad that happened at our house that shows how one of Dad's best quotes came to life in one of the nine lives of our old black-and-white cat.

8

THE QUOTE that got mixed up with Mixy, was one of Dad's newest ones, "Sorrow is knowledge."

I don't suppose Mixy had cat-sense enough to remember what she learned, but it wouldn't be my fault if she didn't—because I was mixed up with Mixy in the very sad experience.

This is the way it happened. My almost-favorite bird around our place is the Robin Redbreast. That spring, as I've already told you, he and his wife had built their nest in the top of our plum tree in a crotch where three branches grew out from the main trunk. It was a perfect place for a robin family. Mom especially enjoyed watching them build it.

Redbreast had been the first bird to come from the South that spring. He and his robin wife had worked hard, gathering clay beside our pump, carrying it in their bills to their house site, mixing it with sticks and grass, actually making a small bowl-shaped nest of mud, before lining it with soft material for the eggs to be laid in and the *altricial* robin babies to be hatched in and to live in, till they reached the fledgling stage. It was very interesting to watch Mrs. Robin—which I did with my binoculars—shaping the mud shell so it would be nice and round and just the right size. She used her light brown body to do it, turning herself 'round and 'round and 'round.

Mixy seemed even more interested in the Robins' house-building than the rest of the Collins family. Every now and then she would come to extra-live life and watch and watch and watch, especially when either one of the robin parents got too close to where she had been sleeping in the sun. One morning, I saw her sneak up close to where Mr. Robin was getting a drink at the kettle under the pump spout and make a quick leap with the greatest of ease straight for Mr. Robin, like there was nothing in the world she would rather have for breakfast than raw robin.

But he was wider awake than anything, and was up on the crossbeam at the east end of the grape arbor in a flash of scared wings. From there he took off for the top of the walnut tree.

Mixy stopped in her tracks, looked up at me with innocent green eyes, as much as to say, "Who cares? That old robin is not fit for a fine cat like me."

One day when Mixy was acting interested again in the *Robins'* family, I spoke sharply to her. "Listen," I said. "You are *not* going to have robin for breakfast or for dinner or for supper! If you *have* to have a meat dinner, get down to the barn and help yourself to those three mice I saw in the granary yesterday!"

She mewed up at me, with her lazy green eyes looking past me at nothing at all, as much as to say,

"Mice? They're not fit for a fine cat like me. It's birds, I'm after."

The days went by, the nest was finished, and Robin and his wife settled down to what Mom called "happy housekeeping."

One day when I climbed up to see how they were getting along, I peeked into the nest and saw four robin's-egg-blue eggs lying in the little round, grass-lined mud cup.

I knew that before long four awkward, very homely, naked little robin babies would be hatched.

Mixy seemed to get lazier and fatter, not showing any interest in mice at all, and not even bothering to do much of anything except lie around in the sun and eat whatever we fed her, Mom seeing to it that she got all she wanted to eat and drink.

Then one morning, when I was standing near the rain barrel, watching baby mosquitoes wriggling in the water, Mom came to the kitchen door and called to me, "What's happened to our robin? He didn't sing me awake this morning, and I haven't seen either one of them!"

"Maybe they've got quadruplets," I said. "I'll climb up and take a look," which I started to do. When I had climbed high enough to look in, there wasn't any mother robin on the nest, and there wasn't even any nest—not any *whole* nest, but just a part of one.

Down on the ground, I looked under the plum tree to see if there were any eggs or baby birds, and there weren't. But there was something else I hadn't seen before, and it was a lot of bird feathers scattered all around, not far from the base of the tree, and one piece of chewed bird wing.

I stood with tears in my eyes, not able to see for a minute, I was so sad; then I felt something warm and furry brushing past my bare legs. Looking down I saw Mixy purring around, sniffing innocently at the feathers and at the piece of chewed bird wing. She blinked up at me, mewed a simpish mew, and started off on a proud, straight-up-tailed walk toward the grape arbor. I couldn't help but notice how extra fat she looked as if she had had a very heavy breakfast of something or other. It was then that the idea struck me. I *knew* what had happened to the robins' nest and to the robin whose feathers were scattered around the base of the plum tree. It was then my thoughts changed to action, and I started with a set jaw toward the grape arbor where Mixy was.

"Sorrow is knowledge," I said to myself. "*Lots* of knowledge! You are going to the head of the class right now, young lady!"

I stooped, picked up a willow switch I'd dropped yesterday—it being safe to leave a switch like that around the place on account of Dad and Mom were using what they called "psychology" on me that year. They hadn't used a single switch on me all summer, and hadn't even needed to.

But psychology wouldn't work on a cat, I decided in a hot-tempered hurry. I picked up the chewed bird wing at the same time I did the switch, and with a very special plan in my mind for Mixy's education, hurried on toward the grape arbor. Mixy had made a big mistake, and she was going to make a big discovery in just about another minute.

I didn't know at the time whether it was Mixy's conscience—if a cat has a conscience—or the switch, that made her a coward, but for some reason I hadn't any sooner started on a businesslike run in her direction, waving the switch in one hand and the chewed bird wing in the other, than she started on a scaredy-cat race for the opened screen door where Mom was, squeezed past Mom's ankles, and disappeared into the kitchen.

With my mind still set on giving Mixy a switching within an inch of her life, I also dived for the screen door, and started to squeeze through past Mom like Mixy had done.

Quick as scat, Mom was all of a sudden in the whole doorway, saying, "Not so fast, young man!"

"Let me through!" I exclaimed to Mom. "That cat's got to learn that sorrow is knowledge. No black-and-white cat's going to climb up into the plum tree, and destroy a robin's nest and kill and eat that robin's only wife!"

I kept on struggling to get past Mom, and couldn't, because Mom was bordered on one side by Charlotte Ann and on the other by a businesslike broom.

Mom's words also blocked the way. Her voice was calm, but very determined, "We don't punish anybody or anything around this farm while we're still very angry. Maybe Mixy tore up the nest and killed and ate Mother Robin, and maybe she didn't. There are other cats in the neighborhood, you know.

And even if she did, she's only a cat; and cats are carnivorous. Carnivorous animals have to have flesh to eat—*raw* flesh. Their systems require it."

"They don't have to tear up birds' nests and eat robins!" I protested, my eyes searching through the screen for a glimpse of Mixy. "Let her eat mice! The granary's full of 'em! If she wasn't too lazy to move out of her tracks to catch even one of them, I'd think more of her! But no! She's too choosy! She has to have beautiful red-breasted bird flesh! She wants to stop beautiful bird songs! She—she—"

Again I tried to squeeze past Mom, and again I got stopped by her broom and by her voice when she said, "Mixy's deserving of a little special love and understanding these days—and a forgiving spirit."

I was still warm-tempered. "I'll forgive her *after* I punish her," I exclaimed.

But Mom got her way, and Mixy went free. The next afternoon, though, I found out why Mom had been so extra careful to keep Mixy from getting punished. I was out gathering eggs at the time. Looking under a loose board in the barn floor where sometimes there was an egg or two in a nest I knew was there, I saw Mixy lying on her side in the place where the nest had been; and lying with her, five of the cutest little shut-eyed, nonsensical-looking baby kittens you ever saw, having their afternoon lunch.

Mixy looked up at me through half-closed green eyes and mewed a proud mew as much as to say, "See there, smarty! This is why your mother wouldn't let you give me a switching yesterday!"

A lump of something came into my throat as I looked down at Mixy, who for the very first time in her life had become a mother. All of a happy sudden, I was very proud of her.

I forgot all about gathering eggs, swung myself off my hands and knees, ducked under the ladder that leads to the haymow, raced past the corner cupboard where Dad keeps his medicines for the stock and his special library of farm books, in a hurry to get to the house to tell Mom about Mixy's new family.

As happy as I was though, and glad about Mixy, as well as proud of her, I was still remembering the sad feeling I had had yesterday when I climbed up into the plum tree and saw the robins' nest all torn up and realized the mother robin had been killed and eaten. It was probably somebody's stray cat that had wandered into the neighborhood, maybe some friend of Mixy's, I thought.

* * *

There was a lot of sorrow that week for some of the people who lived over in Halifax county. Vandals not only burned a cross in Ballard's yard just outside his door, but they had thrown rocks at his house and broken quite a few of his windows.

To frighten them away, Sam had fired two shotgun blasts out into the night, being careful, Dad found out, to shoot straight up in the air, so nobody would get hurt.

The vandals came back the next night and pushed over one of Sam's small outbuildings, and they did the same thing to several white families in the neighborhood.

All that week, while our friendly tenant was living in our tree house, I felt fine that our gang was being kind to him. For a while it looked like Dragonfly was going to get rid of some of his graveclothes, when one morning he came up with an idea. "Why doesn't he move into a real motel like other people. The Green Corn could stand a little more business!"

Imagine that! We were all lying on the grass in the shade of the Little Jim Tree at the time. Dragonfly was chewing on the soft end of a stalk of timothy grass he had just pulled, which a boy likes to do, because of the crisp, sweetish taste of the timothy grass.

"He has two more days before his week is up," I reminded Dragonfly, still surprised at his changed attitude.

Little Jim piped up with a question, "Is Shorty still staying at the Green Corn?"

Dragonfly stifled a sneeze, sighed, and answered, "They had to move. They had the double unit right next to the office, which is where I sleep, and I was allergic to the paint he was using. I have to sneeze enough as it is."

I got another surprise when Dragonfly came out with, "I don't like Shorty anymore."

"How come?" Circus asked, and Dragonfly answered, "He's too uppity about black people. He fooled me into putting those signs at the spring and at our tree house. He even charged me fifty cents apiece for them, but when Mr. Robinson came over to see Dad and Mother and offered to pay them extra rent because the tree house was on our property, I knew black people were not all bad, like Shorty said they were!"

Dragonfly finished with a heavy sigh, then added, "I don't see how I could have been such a dumb bunny. I should have remembered what a fool he made out of me that summer when he almost broke up our gang."

For several minutes, not a one of us said a word. Then Big Jim looked at Dragonfly and asked, "Want to tell us about Mr. Robinson's visit?"

And Dragonfly did. It happened on an evening when the Gilberts' No Vacancy sign was on, and they had seven units with nobody in them, and Dragonfly's parents were feeling pretty sad, when the old man came hobbling into the court. He'd noticed, he told them, that their boy was having difficulty breathing, and he wondered if they had heard about a new asthma medicine that was helping a lot of people.

I don't know how the old man found out the Gilberts had money problems, but he told them he'd saved quite a lot of money through the years, and if they'd let him he'd like to use some of it to help their son.

Dragonfly finished his story, and when I looked at him, there were actual tears in his eyes. "Shorty Long is wrong!" he said with his fists doubled up. "Black people are *not* all bad."

Then Dragonfly looked at his wristwatch, and at

the late afternoon sun, and said, "I've got to get home." He picked up his thermos jug, scrambled to his feet, and took off. He'd been carrying his thermos for about a week now, because he didn't weigh enough, and their family doctor had ordered him to drink chocolate milk between meals, so he could gain weight and maybe have better health.

Ragweed season would come in a little over a month, and if Dragonfly was stronger, he might be able to live through it without having so much asthma.

As I watched the little guy's thin legs carrying him on a fast trot across the battleground of the battle of Bumblebee Hill, on his way to his dad's cornfield in the direction of the Green Corn Motel, I had a warm feeling in my heart toward him. He had been made a fool of by a bigger, meaner boy, and maybe we ought not to blame him too much for getting all mixed up in his mind toward a lot of things, like that other summer when Shorty Long took over and ran him like a boy riding a motorcycle.

Big Jim spoke then, and what he said made me feel even kinder toward Roy Gilbert. "I'd like somebody to make a motion that we use the rent we've received for our Tree House Motel to help the Gilberts pay for Dragonfly's allergy treatments."

Big Jim looked around at his little circle of gang members, and all of a sudden everyone of us said at almost the same time, "I so move."

I reached over and broke off a stalk of ragweed that was growing at the base of the Little Jim Tree.

It wouldn't be long now before it would start to flower, and the pollen of a million weeds like it would start flying all over everywhere, making Dragonfly's nose and eyes water, and making it hard for him to breathe. Even his bronchial tubes would swell shut—or almost, anyway—and he would have a hard time being glad to be alive.

That night, there was more vandalism, some of it pretty bad. It was in the newspapers now, and on the radio. One of the very worst things some twisted-minded boys had done was to upset a half dozen of the tombstones in one of the town cemeteries.

"Vandalism Sweeping the County," was on the very front page of the Sugar Creek *Times* when I took it out of the mailbox the next morning.

My heart was pounding as I read it. What if some rough boys should find out about Benjamin Robin son living in our tree house, and do something mean to him! What if vandalism should get started right in our own neighborhood.

I started on a fast run toward the house with the mail, passing the plum tree, where a few bird feathers still were scattered, and on toward the kitchen door.

"Here's the mail!" I cried to Mom, handing her the *Times* and a letter from Memory City, Indiana, which would be from my cousin Wally's mother, Dad's red-haired sister. I called her my "Red Ant."

Mom's eyes lit up when she saw the letter—getting a letter being one of the most important things that ever happens to Mom, and *not* getting one being one of the worst.

But I wasn't happy. I was worried, thinking, *What if something* had *happened to Mr. Robinson last night!*

I left Mom reading the letter, and scurried out across the yard, leaving the gate open like a forgetful gentleman, raced across the graveled road, squeezed through the rail fence, and a few jiffies later was flying down the little brown path toward the spring—not like a scared cottontail with a hound on his trail, but like a hound, myself, hot on the trail of some vandalism, if there was any.

When I reached the clearing in sight of our tree house, I stopped, my heart pounding from what I saw. The vandalism *had* spread to Sugar Creek!

Our tree house looked like it had been struck by a cyclone; it was twisted all out of shape, with dried grass and sedge scattered all over, the entrance pushed into a ridiculous angle, making it too small for anybody to squeeze through to get in; the captain's chair was upside down, and the old man's belongings were in a helter-skelter mess over the little knoll.

Then I spotted something that made my whole body cringe! Lying near the outdoor fireplace we'd built for the old man, was his artificial leg, twisted and trampled into the ground, like a bird wing somebody's cat had chewed on and left there all by itself.

The old man himself was gone!

9

I STOOD LOOKING through my tears at our torn-up tree house: at the strips of canvas that had been a part of the roof, the bare ribs of the old lawn umbrella, the broken-down cot that had been the old man's bed, the marsh grass all over the place.

The feeling that stormed into my mind was like a cyclone, I was so furious at what had been done and at who ever had done it.

As quick as Old Bawler leaps into a fight with a coon, I started on the run toward the center of the scattered house, where I stopped, swooped up the old man's artificial leg, which, I was surprised to find out, was almost as light as a feather. It was made out of some very light metal, was jointed at the knee and ankle, and was finished with enamel. The old man's shoe was still on the foot. It felt very strange, like I was carrying an actual part of a human being's body.

A jiffy later I was running again, past the beech tree with all the initials carved on it, past the garbage can that always was there for picnickers to put their trash in, and was racing through the woods toward home. The faster I ran in that little brown path, the worse I felt, just the opposite of the way I usually feel when I am running there, when a very happy feeling goes racing along inside of me.

I swished past the white foam flowers and wild strawberries and sweetbriers like they weren't even there, and their fragrance that sometimes made me almost sick it was so sweet, didn't seem like anything, I was so full of sadness.

Plop—plop—plop—scrunch—scrunch—scrunch—my feet keeping time to something Dad had been quoting that summer as I flew along, "Sorrow is knowledge. Sorrow is knowledge. Sorrow is knowledge.

When I was through the gate at the walnut tree at our house, I raced across the yard, passing the plum tree where part of Robin Redbreast's nest still lay scattered, past the pump, yanked open the screen door to the kitchen, hurried through, burst into the living room where Mom was, and with tears in my eyes and voice, told her what had happened.

I must have looked astonishing to Mom, standing flush-faced and excited, holding the old stranger's artificial leg in my arms, like a jointed piece of wood I'd carried in for the kitchen stove.

I was mixed up in my mind, which is why my tongue got a little twisted in what I was saying, as I sort of sobbed out to her, "They—they-they—somebody's stray cat—I mean somebody has torn down our tree house and scattered it all over everywhere, and—and—and has done something terrible to Mr. Robinson; and all that's left of him is one leg, and I don't know where the rest of him is and—"

I didn't get to finish my sentence, because my

mind got interrupted when I saw through the east window somebody coming through the front gate—a bareheaded old man, with white hair and long white whiskers. "Look!" I cried to Mom. "It's Old Man Paddler! He's home from his vacation!"

Nearly always, when I have seen that kind long-whiskered old man in the woods or anywhere, he is going kind of slow because he can't see well anymore and has arthritis in his knees and ankles and quite often uses a cane.

But this time he was in a hurry, like he was excited about something.

Mom and I reached the side door just as the old man himself did. He could hardly wait to get through the screen Mom was holding open for him, and he was panting for breath, he exclaimed, "Quick, Mrs. Collins! Phone Dr. Manswood! There's a sick man down at the mouth of the cave! I think he's having a heart attack!"

Mom was like a skirted arrow on her way to the phone.

I certainly felt helpless, standing there with the old man's leg in my arms. I thought I knew who the sick man at the mouth of the cave was, but I wanted to be sure, so I asked Old Man Paddler, "Is-is he a black man with only one leg?"

It seemed Old Man Paddler noticed me then for the first time. I could see the puzzled expression in his eyes, as he looked at what I had in my arms. Then he answered me with a worried voice, nodding his grizzled old head at the same time, "That's right!"

Hearing him say that, I knew that the person having a heart attack at the mouth of the cave was our very own tenant. I knew also that somebody had to do something to help save his life quick, *before* the doctor could get there.

"Here, hold this!" I exclaimed to Old Man Paddler. I handed him the artificial leg, swung around to the work table near the sink, grasped a clean milk bottle Mom had just washed and put there, and shot out the door to the pump.

The bottle pumped full, I circled the ivy trellis that shades the side porch and the kitchen's side door and yelled in through the front room's open window to Mom at the phone, "Tell Dr. Manswood to come to the cave! We'll be there, waiting!"

I was going to be a doctor someday myself, when and if I ever grew up. As I raced to the Collins' front gate, it seemed like I was already a doctor, answering an emergency call. The milk bottle filled with fresh water was my doctor's bag. If there was anything in the world I wouldn't want to happen, it was that the kind old stranger would die before he could put up a tombstone for his mother and his twin baby brother.

He's got to live! He's got *to!* I thought desperately. It seemed my bare feet were filled with lead, although I could tell I was running fast by the wind in my face, and the way my shirt sleeves were flapping.

Reaching the corner where the graveled road turns north, I shot past the three big maple trees and on toward the bridge.

At the bridge, I swung off the road and up the grade to the left, squeezed through the rail fence at the top, and galloped on, following the ridge above the creek. In another few minutes I'd be at the mouth of the branch. At the branch I'd cross on the log bridge and be on the last lap to the sycamore tree and the cave.

Panting—panting—panting—

In a little while, I, Bill Collins, the doctor, would be there. I'd find the old man lying with his crutches beside him in the shade of the sycamore, gasping for breath, and with the water I was taking to him for the pill he would have to have, I'd save his life.

For some reason as I flew along in the path, leaping over fallen trees, dodging shrubbery and stumps, I was remembering Lincoln's Gettysburg address, which we'd had to memorize in school, and which has a line in it that says, "All men are created equal."

With every step, the word "equal" repeated itself in my mind.

"Equal—equal—equal—equal"

My thoughts were interrupted just then by somebody behind me, yelling, "Hey, Bill! Wait for me!"

It was Dragonfly's high-pitched voice.

"I can't," I yelled back over my shoulder to him. I also *looked* over my shoulder, which means that for a few seconds my eyes were not on the path I was supposed to be running in; also that I didn't see the ponderosa pine tree root sticking up several inches in the path. The next thing I knew, I was in the middle of a head-over-heels tumble, with my right big toe feeling like it had been struck with a hammer, and my right ankle hurting with one of the worst pains I'd ever felt in my life.

I landed upside down outside the path beside a sweetbrier bush. I knew it was that kind of bush because I was smelling the flowers, and also because I had been scratched on my face and arms when I fell, landing partly in, partly on and partly under the sharp-thorned rose bush.

But I was still holding onto the milk bottle and only a little of the water had been spilled.

Dragonfly caught up with me then, but I could hardly see him I was so dizzy with the pain in my toe and ankle.

" 'Smatter?" he asked me.

I rolled over and up to a sitting position. I tried to get up all the way, and did; but when I started to walk, my ankle hurt even worse, and I went down in a pile of pain.

"Quick!" I gasped to Dragonfly. "Help me up! I have to get to him to save his life! He's down by the sycamore tree at the mouth of the cave and has to have a drink of water so he can take his pill, or he might die!"

"What's the matter with who?" Dragonfly asked, his voice whiny.

"Mr. Robinson! He's having a heart attack! Help me up!"

Dragonfly did help me up, but I couldn't run; I couldn't even walk, and I knew I'd never be able to hop on one foot all the way to the cave. "You'll have to take it to him yourself," I exclaimed to

Dragonfly, who just that minute got a mussed-up expression on his face, and let out two fast sneezes.

"Take what to *who*?" He couldn't seem to get it into his head what I meant and whose life he was supposed to help save.

"Old Mr. Robinson!" I told him impatiently. "He's got to have a drink of water! You've got to take it to him yourself!"

I looked at my twisted foot for a second, and a frightened feeling shot through me. Maybe I'd been hurt so badly I'd have to wear an artificial leg myself!

Dragonfly's puckered face and the branches of the ponderosa pine above him began to whirl, and it seemed like a million mixed-up thoughts were racing 'round and 'round in my mind: Mixy with her tail straight up was marching proudly across the yard with a dead robin in her mouth, the robin right away changing into a baby kitten; then five baby kittens were lying beside Mixy in a hen's nest under a loose board in the barn floor; our tree house was torn down and scattered all over everywhere by an African lion, which had just finished eating all of Mr. Robinson except one leg, which he *couldn't* eat because it was made of some kind of metal.

Then it seemed like I was falling. Down—down—down—

The next thing I knew, I felt cold water being splashed into my face and heard Dragonfly's nervous voice crying, "Bill! Wake up and tell me *whose* life has got to be saved, and where is he?"

At first I couldn't remember anything clearly,

then I came to, and told him that Mr. Robinson was having a heart attack down by the sycamore tree at the mouth of the cave. "He always takes a pill when he's having one, and it revives him. But he hasn't got any water. You've got to get some to him! It's in the milk bottle, there—there—"

My eyes searched frantically for the bottle, as I struggled to a sitting position. Then I saw the bottle lying in the shade of the sweetbrier bush, and it was empty! *Empty!*

Dragonfly had used the water to revive *me!* He'd splashed every drop of it on my face and neck to bring me out of my faint!

There wasn't any water left for the old man, not even enough for him to swallow a pill!

What to do now!

I was surprised that there was hardly any pain in my ankle and toe, and there was only a warm feeling instead; then I remembered that once last year when I'd hit my thumb with a hammer, there had been at first a rush of pain that had made me sick at my stomach and very faint, but about two minutes later there had been only a warm feeling in my thumb and hand. The worst of the pain was gone and it never came back.

The pain in my toe and ankle might be gone for good, too. I still might be able to get some water to the old man *if* I could find any that would be safe to drink, which this time of year Sugar Creek water wouldn't be, nor branch water either.

Then I spied Dragonfly's thermos bottle, and an

idea came to me. Maybe the old man could take his pill with chocolate milk.

"Do you have chocolate milk in your thermos?"

"I've got cold water. I got it at the spring after I finished my milk. You need some more in your face? You still feel faint?" Dragonfly in a dumb minute, not still seeming to realize the desperate situation, started to unscrew the thermos cap.

I made a grab for it, took it away from him, and came to still faster life as I said, "I can save his life with this," and was off on a limping run toward the mouth of the branch.

"Save *whose* life?" that slow-to-catch-on little rascal asked me, and I yelled back over my shoulder, "I *told* you! Ben Robinson's! He's having a heart attack at the sycamore tree by the mouth of the cave!"

I was all the way to the log bridge at the mouth of the branch before Dragonfly caught up with me again.

With every limping step, while Dragonfly was chasing me, it seemed I was fighting something in my mind. *Why*, I kept asking myself, *is he so stubborn! Doesn't he want the old man to live! Has he been just pretending to be a changed boy? Does he still think like Shorty Long! Maybe he doesn't even think a black man has a right to drink out of a white boy's thermos bottle!*

In my mind's eye, I was seeing the two signs at the spring, and the other one in the captain's chair at our tree house. Dragonfly admitted that he had put the signs there but had blamed Shorty Long for talking him into doing it.

And then I came back into my right mind and remembered I was a doctor rushing to save a man's life, and in a jiffy had limped my way acoss the log bridge to the other side, with Dragonfly right behind me.

My ankle still wouldn't behave right, and I felt sharp pain in every step, as I struggled down the path ahead of Dragonfly.

We weren't far from the cave now. I could see the trunk of the big sycamore, with its white, purple and gray patches of bark, and I knew that somewhere down on the ground there was the old man we still might be able to save.

Things began to whirl in front of my eyes. I felt my knees buckling and my self going down like I had before. I was going to faint again. I knew it, and I couldn't help it.

Even as I started to go down, face-first, I glimpsed Dragonfly's blue-overalled, spindle-legged self breaking out into the open, his flying feet carrying him farther and farther away, taking the thermos bottle with him.

10

QUITE A FEW THINGS happened while I was lying there, not knowing anything. I had several important surprises when I came to.

The first thing I realized, I was lying on my back having cold water sprinkled in my face again. The first thing I *saw* was the worried face of Dragonfly Gilbert. He was kneeling in the grass beside me. In one of his hands he had the thermos bottle, and was pouring water from it into his other hand and sprinkling the water on my face and neck.

Mr. Robinson was there, also, alive and all right. The first thing I heard was his quavering voice, "He's coming to,"—meaning I was regaining consciousness, and was in my mind again.

Several other people were there, also: Old Man Paddler, Dr. Manswood, and Mom, with Charlotte Ann standing beside her, wide-eyed and grinning at me like she was tickled to see me, and thought her big half-homely brother was a very nice person.

I should have known Charlotte Ann better than that, though, because when I started to get up, and was on my hands and knees halfway, she broke loose from Mom and flew into fast action, her bare feet carrying her like a mischievous little chipmunk toward me.

Before I realized what was happening, that little rascal of a baby sister was climbing on my shoulders for a piggyback ride!

It could have been a happy time for me if Dragonfly hadn't been so proud of himself. Mr. Robinson who was *really* feeling fine again and breathing like a well person, braced himself against the white and purple and gray trunk of the sycamore tree, laid his hand on Dragonfly's thin shoulder and said, "This boy saved my life. He brought me a drink of water just in time."

I looked at Dragonfly, and even before his voice said what his mind was thinking, I read it on his crooked-nosed face. This is what that little rascal of a dumb bunny actually said: "I gave him a drink out of my thermos bottle."

Even Mom didn't know any better, because she said to Dragonfly—my own mother, mind you!—"I always knew you were alert. You stop at the house after a while for a piece of peach pie I baked just this morning."

Dr. Manswood, after examining my ankle, decided I'd have to stay off it for a while, for a few days anyway. Mom got worried then, and when the doctor had driven me home in his car, she took care of me *extra* carefully, as if I had been Roy "Dragonfly" Gilbert, himself, the life-saving hero!

Another thing Dr. Manswood did, was to take Mr. Robinson to his office and give him a very special examination and change his medicine. He gave him a new kind of pill he could take without water. All he had to do was slip the pill under his tongue and let it dissolve. It would give very fast relief to a person with his kind of heart trouble. I found out about it later.

Before we left the cave, though, there was a big surprise, especially for Old Man Paddler when he found out who the old stranger was. I saw the long-whiskered old white man give the long whiskered old black man a hearty handshake and an actual hug, exclaiming "So you're Benjamin Robinson!"

I found out later that Old Man Paddler had been sending money to the mission board, helping to support Mr. Robinson, but had kept his gifts secret, Old Man Paddler liking to give that way for some reason.

Anyway, because our Weaverbird Motel couldn't be lived in anymore, Old Man Paddler asked the retired missionary to stay at his house, a clapboard-roofed cabin in the hills.

As I started to say, Mom gave me and my ankle very special care, like I was even more important than Dragonfly had made himself seem. You could see, though, that she was a little suspicious of the story of Dragonfly's having saved Mr. Robinson's life, by the tone of her voice when she asked, just as she finished wrapping a cold, wet towel around my ankle, "Roy is quite a hero, isn't he?"

"Quite," I grunted.

Dad, who was at the water pail in the corner getting a drink, remarked, "Quite a change from the Dragonfly of last week."

I had my eyes buried in a book on first aid, checking to see if what the doctor had ordered for my ankle was right—and it was. I answered Dad with a tone of voice he didn't like very well when I said, "It was a good chance for him to show off a little."

"You couldn't possibly be a little jealous because you didn't get to do what *he* did?" Dad asked.

Mom put in then, saying, "There seems to be part of the story missing. The milk bottle, for instance. You know where it is?"

"Ask Dragonfly," I answered, with the same wrong tone of voice. "He poured water out of it onto my face to bring me out of my *first* faint. I fainted twice, you know."

"Good boy!" Dad said. But I didn't get a chance to feel proud of myself for being able to come to *twice* in one afternoon, because he wasn't talking about me, but about a boy named Dragonfly Gilbert. I wasn't even glad about what Dad said next. "Somebody has done a good job snipping off the graveclothes he was wrapped in only a week or so ago."

I wasn't sure Dragonfly was set free. It still seemed like he had just changed one kind of graveclothes for another; first, he'd been wrapped 'round and 'round with race prejudice, and now he was wrapped 'round and 'round with the thought that he was a big hero. It still seemed like the only reason he had changed his attitude toward Ben Robinson was that Shorty Long had moved out of the Green Corn Motel and wasn't there anymore to control his wishy-washy mind. Also, he hated to be on the outs with the gang.

I didn't find out for sure that he was a changed boy until some time later, when the gang was having a special meeting in the cemetery near Sarah Paddler's tombstone. All of us except Circus, were in for quite a surprise.

One reason we'd planned our meeting for the cemetery was that the day before while I was up in our haymow—being able to walk on my ankle again, and to climb the haymow stairs if I would be careful—I looked out the always-open east window, which Dad calls his "picture window," and noticed a truck with two men in it driving down the far side of the cemetery, following the grass-grown lane inside the rock fence Poetry and I had been hiding behind on that important day you already know about.

The truck had stayed in the cemetery quite a while, maybe two hours, before it came back and went east up the graveled road leading toward town.

I hadn't thought anything about it, on account of just three days before had been Memorial Day, and quite a few people had gone through the cemetery, following the little brown paths and leaving flags or flowers or potted plants at different people's graves—a few soldiers of the Civil War having been buried there. Memorial Day, the same as Decoration Day, was always on May 30th in our part of the United States.

Wondering if maybe the men in the truck had done some special work there, such as cutting grass away from different stones, or something, or maybe even putting up a new headstone for somebody, I thought maybe the gang would like to know about it, so I phoned Poetry who phoned Circus who phoned Little Jim who phoned Big Jim who was supposed to phone Dragonfly, and didn't on account of the Gilberts' phone was out of order. We would meet first at the Little Jim Tree, everybody was supposed to tell everybody. The meeting was for Sunday afternoon at two o'clock.

Sunday morning, we went to church like our family had been doing ever since I was old enough to be carried there. We hadn't seen very much of Benjamin Robinson since he had moved up to Old Man Paddler's, so it seemed good to see him that Sunday morning in church. Little Jim's folks had driven up into the hills to get the two old men, since it was a long way for them to have to walk at their age, being the oldest old men in the whole territory.

When Mr. Robinson came limping in, I got a warm feeling in my heart. I had had to use crutches a few days myself, and still had a little limp. Right that very second, I was wearing an elastic bandage on my ankle.

The church was almost full of all kinds of people, some of them being tourists who were on early vacations.

We had already sung the first hymn, "Blest Be the Tie that Binds," and were sitting down, when Circus' Dad who was an usher that year, came down the outside west aisle ahead of Old Man Paddler and

Ben Robinson, and seated them in the same pew with the Gilbert family.

The sermon was something about Memorial Day, and soldiers and the Civil War and the Memorial of the Lord's Supper. Every time we held communion, we were sort of decorating the grave of the Saviour, even though He hadn't stayed there, but was alive. The best way to decorate His grave was to live a clean, honest life, as if we had come out of the grave of sin ourselves.

Part of the sermon was about the cross, and how it was more important to have the cross in your heart than to have it on the church steeple, or to wear it as a lapel pin. "The Christian cross is aflame today with the love of God. It lights the darkness in the human heart and helps every person of every race to see himself a sinner in need of the Saviour."

Just as our pastor said those words, I was reminded of the little pocket mirror I always carried with me, and taking it out, I looked on the back where the printed words were:

Christ died for the sinner.
Which One?
See the other side.

Like I always do when I read those words, I looked on the other side, and saw a freckle-faced, red-haired boy named William Jasper Collins.

And then I got a very cheerful surprise, for while I was looking in the mirror, I saw behind me, upstairs in the front row of the balcony the Ballard family, all seven of them. They were listening with serious faces, and I knew that maybe all of them were remembering another flaming cross that had burned outside their house, and the expression on Sam Ballard's face said he wasn't mad at anybody for hating his family, but he was sorry for them that they didn't understand about the real cross, nor love the One who had died on it for the sins of everybody.

It was a very hot, sultry day, and without knowing I was going to do it, because as a certain poem says, "No boy knows when he goes to sleep," I drifted off into the land of Wynken, Blynken, and Nod, and missed most of the rest of the sermon.

I came to with a jerk when our pastor announced a hymn, and people all around me started leafing through their hymn books.

And then came two more surprises. First, our pastor announced we had a retired missionary in the audience. He asked Ben Robinson to stand for everybody to see him, Old Man Paddler standing with him because he was a special guest of that kind old man.

The other surprise came while we were singing the closing hymn. I heard a very pretty contralto voice from somewhere behind me. I turned my head quick-like and found it was Miss Trillium who was visiting our church that day. Her face was very happy, and I felt sure her thoughts were, *All human beings are the handwriting of God. The Creator writes with different colored inks.*

And just like it had been that morning in school when she had told it to us, it seemed like the Creator was in our church in a very special way. I was sorry I had let the hot weather make me sleepy and that I had missed part of the sermon. I didn't get to find out *what* I'd missed until the gang's meeting that afternoon.

We met first at the Little Jim Tree—all of us except Dragonfly, who hadn't been meeting with us lately anyway, on account of we all still didn't feel very friendly toward him, and he seemed afraid to come over to any of our houses.

One thing we had found out for sure was that he was *not* the person who had torn down our tree house; some evil-minded vandals had. From the Little Jim Tree, we lazied across the battleground of the battle of Bumblebee Hill and on up to the cemetery where at Sarah Paddler's grave we all stopped and stared at what we saw. There were *three* tombstones there instead of just two. We'd seen the *two* many a time. One, as you know, was Sarah Paddler's, Old Man Paddler's wife who had been dead a long time; the other was for the old man himself. Of course, Old Man Paddler was still alive, but he had had his stone put up ahead of time with his name on it and the date of his birth. There was a vacant place on the stone where somebody someday would have to put in the date of his death.

The thing that had stopped us was a brand-new marker, a little different in shape, shining in the sun just a few feet from the others.

Little Jim spoke first, piping up with a question: "How come there isn't any mound of fresh earth, if somebody's been just buried here?"

"Yeah," I said, "how come?" I was remembering the truck I'd seen driving down inside the stone fence yesterday.

We all found out "how come?" when we saw the words on the new tombstone, which were:

ELIZABETH ROBINSON
Runaway Slave
Set free forever through the blood of Christ.

Just below were two dates, one for when she was born and the other for when she died. Just below the dates was a small baby lamb, and below it, two of the saddest words I'd ever seen anywhere. They were:

LITTLE BENNY

We all sort of came to, and Circus told us, "The actual grave is over there just *outside* the rail fence under the blackberry bushes. I know because I helped Mr. Robinson measure the distances on his map. Old Man Paddler wanted the tombstone put up *inside* the cemetery and on his own family lot. That's how come it's here."

"Listen!" Poetry whispered to us. "Somebody's coming."

And somebody was. I knew *who* when I heard, about forty yards away, a long-tailed, wheezy sneeze.

Quicker'n five chipmunks we obeyed Big Jim's order to hide.

A few seconds later we were all over the stone fence and crouched down out of sight. I peeped between two stones and saw Dragonfly carrying a bonquet of flowers in a milk bottle.

Dragonfly stood where we had a little while before and looked at the new stone and what was on it—only, he kept on standing with the bottle of flowers in his hands.

He looked all around, as if he wanted to be sure nobody was seeing him, then he carried his bouquet to the new tombstone, set it down carefully, just below the lamb and the words "Little Benny."

I could hardly believe my eyes, even though I couldn't see too well, on account of I was watching through the crack between the stones, and the leaves of a sweetbrier bush on the other side kept blowing across my peephole. Right that second, Little Jim, who was beside me trying to peek over the top of the fence so he could see too, accidentally knocked a rock loose.

The rock made a scatching sound, as it fell off the wall on the other side of the fence and rolled toward the pine tree near Sarah Paddler's tombstone.

Dragonfly jumped like he had heard a shot, whirled around, and ran like a scared cottontail toward the other side of the cemetery, not stopping until he had reached the rail fence, where he crawled through and disappeared.

When, a little later, we were all back in front of the new gravestone, not a one of us said a word for what seemed like a long time. Poetry was the first to say anything. "History," he said, "has repeated itself." Then he quoted part of a poem, which I will quote here for you, and which makes a nice way to end this story—just before I dive headfirst into the next one.

> No more shall the war cry sever,
> Or the winding rivers be red;
> They banish our anger forever
> When they laurel the graves of our dead.

The civil war in the Sugar Creek Gang was over, and we were all going to be friends again.

Little Jim came up with a suggestion which was just like him, when he said, "I move we go hunt up Dragonfly and tell him."

Big Jim's answer was, "The motion is carried."

He hadn't even waited for anybody to second the motion, nor bothered to ask us to vote. There wasn't a one of us that wasn't willing to forgive Dragonfly. He had banished our anger forever when he had decorated the grave of Mr. Robinson's mother and his twin brother, Little Benny.

Big Jim's answer was ringing in my ears as all five of us started off on a fast barefoot race in a topsy-turvy direction toward the place where we'd last seen Dragonfly.

I had to run pretty carefully on my still-bandaged ankle. I was glad I didn't have to use crutches or wear an artificial limb, and I was feeling fine inside that Dragonfly's rebellion was over.

As we raced along, all kinds of butterflies and dragonflies were everywhere on the lazy afternoon air. The smell of wild flowers was enough to make a boy dizzy—in fact, it seemed like everything in nature had a pure heart—even the dragonflies.

That night at the supper table, Dad surprised Mom and me by saying, "I stopped at the Gilberts this afternoon—and guess what?"

When neither Mom nor I could guess what, Dad cleared his throat like he sometimes does when he is about to say something extra important, and announced, "Ben Robinson has just moved into unit twelve and is going to stay for a week. I think I never saw LeRoy and Lilly so happy."

I was still a little bothered about Dragonfly having gotten the credit for saving the old man's life, so I asked, "What about LeRoy's son? Was he happy about it?"

Dad quick looked at me as if I shouldn't have asked such a question, then he used his teaching voice to say, "Never judge any person by what he was yesterday—if he is a *new* man today."

Just that minute, from outdoors somewhere there came the cheerful whistle of Mom's favorite bird, the cardinal, and it seemed like instead of whistling, Cheer! Cheer! Cheer! he was calling, Peace! Peace! Peace!

It also seemed like my mother was answering him, when she looked across the corner of the table at the world's best father, and said, "God is still on the throne."

Charlotte Ann didn't even know what was going on in our minds, because right that minute she finished her chocolate milk and held out her cup for more.